THE UNICORN, THE MYSTERY

The Unicorn, The Mystery

A novel
by

JANET MASON

BOOKS

Adelaide Books
New York / Lisbon
2020

THE UNICORN, THE MYSTERY
A novel
By Janet Mason

Copyright © by Janet Mason
Cover design © 2020 Adelaide Books

Published by Adelaide Books, New York / Lisbon
adelaidebooks.org

Editor-in-Chief
Stevan V. Nikolic

For any information, please address Adelaide Books
at info@adelaidebooks.org
or write to:
Adelaide Books
244 Fifth Ave. Suite D27
New York, NY, 10001

ISBN: 978-1-953510-25-9

Printed in the United States of America

In memory of my mother and father, S. Jane Mason and Albert Mason, who led me to the Cloisters, and to my partner Barbara (a.k.a. Foxx) and to my faith community at the Unitarian Universalist Church of the Restoration.

Chapter One

"There is too much blood."

The child pointed to the bright red blood dripping down my otherwise pure white side – and to the gash my horn had gouged in the side of the hunting dog. I do not normally hurt other animals – or humans for that matter – but the hound belonged to the hunters who had trapped and cornered me with their long javelins.

"That man is bad. I can see it in his eyes," continued the child.

The child had a point. The man's eyes are flat and glittering. Even as he points his javelin toward my head, you know that this kill – if it comes to pass – will not be enough for him. He will want more. I can see this but even now I still wonder – why would anyone want to capture me? Why didn't they just leave me alone? Was I that important?

To distract myself from being bored, I watch the groups of people that pass through this room.

Today, the most interesting person in the room is small and is wearing a shiny and long magenta dress. I've heard little girls so adorned called princesses. Really, they are imitating a time long gone, and they are re-living a myth. It's true that in my day princesses lived in castles. But little girls were not passive. They had to be bred to be passive. The myth-makers thought that they would make future little girls passive through the repetition of fairy tales. But young women did not dangle their long blond locks from towers and wait for the handsome prince to come and save them. They did not sit beautiful behind locked doors, waiting to be rescued. They may have had to do it in secret, but many princesses developed their muscles. They learned to use javelins, shields and spears. They unleashed their power – even though they were frequently opposed and overpowered. I hear the tradition continues – despite the myth. This little princess may free me from the tapestry to tell you my story. Just remember that it is a real story – not a fairy tale.

I am going to start in the middle of the story of how they captured me. I've always wondered myself. How was it possible? Part of my legend and lure was that it was impossible to capture me. But this was not always true. People have hunted my kind for many reasons. They may have claimed that they were chasing my horn which they fancied as imbued with all types of powers. My horn was said to be a cure-all for everything, including mortality – as if that could be cured. They were especially keen on insisting that a ground-up horn from my kind acted as an antidote to poison. This was an untruth of course. Everything was false. They were chasing that which cannot be caught.

Let me start at the beginning – or rather in the middle. Of course, I defended myself. What other choice did I have? I see in this tapestry, that I am cornered and there is blood. But I am still surrounded by beauty. There is a stream flowing in front of me. Another day, I would have bent my head, lowered the tip of my horn into the stream, and cleansed it so the other animals could drink.

There are a few birds: the common gray goshawk, the noble falcon with its long wings who is not taking any notice of the hunters behind me as it stares down at the stream; and several types of ducks, including the mallard with its regal white ring circling its neck. Far in the background, at the top of the tapestry, is the pomegranate tree I have just eaten a ripe fruit from before I wandered away. To tell you the truth I was savoring some fermented fruits on the ground – which always makes me feel a little giddy. That may be why I didn't see the hunters come up behind me until it was almost too late.

My hindquarters raised, I was poised to jump over the stream. The person who did the drawing for the tapestry maker caught me between galloping away and the moment when I realized that I had to give a swift kick, with both of my rear legs, to the hunter behind me. He was so close that I could feel the steely wind from his javelin on my rear quarters. As I mentioned, I am not usually aggressive. But I do like to be alone. It seemed that these hunters – suddenly surrounding me, with their javelins, bugles, and dogs – wanted to disturb my solitude and more.

I am surrounded by flowers: white lilies, wild red roses, St. Mary's thistle and my favorite, the pungent stock gillyflower. I can smell their mingled sweet and spicy scent. I see the blurred colors of lavender, pink and white as I gallop by. Nonetheless, I could still tell that the throng of hunters, that was gaining on me, meant to do me harm.

Now that I have time to really look at the scene depicted in this tapestry, I see that most of the men wear brown cloaks atop red tunics. Three of the men wear shiny blue cloaks crinkled like crushed velvet. All are wearing hats – more than a few are red, others brown — perched on their heads. One man, standing in the back, the man with a bugle hanging on him, wears a fancy red hat with a feather plume curling up from the brim. He holds his javelin straight up with the wooden pole near the ground. He looks down like he is musing. A poet, perhaps? He appears to be someone who thinks he is above the fray. Given his fancy dress – and the fact that there was always a hierarchy, he could be a representative of the King. It is said that the King represents God. If it is true – as I've heard it said – that I was a symbol of the son of God, then why would He want me captured? Wouldn't He want me left alone to be part of the beauty of nature? There is so much in this world that doesn't make sense.

I remember being in the grounds of the abbey. I was drawn there because there seems to be more room for solitude. The village inside the stone walls of the abbey was quieter and the people more contemplative. There was a church and a pig trough. The well was frequently unattended, so I could drink to my heart's delight. There were more likely to be virginal maidens here – especially in the nun's quarters – than other places. In the village that I had to pass through to get here, there were no virginal maidens at all. I had wandered into the burial ground, thinking that I could find some solitude. But then I had to flee from the people living there in makeshift tents and women plying their wares – and I do mean *all* of their wares.

At the top left of the tapestry, behind the trees, the cherry, the pomegranate, the walnut, the bushy oak, is a castle in miniature. On the middle tower, a red triangular roof that appears tiny in the distance flies an equally small flag, a triangle with a point on the end. Perhaps the castle is within view of the abbey to remind the holy ones – even the Bishop – that they work for the King.

I admit that I was afraid of the hunters. I was especially concerned about their intent to invade my solitude. But I was not fearful of going to the castle, because I heard that the princess there – the king's only daughter – was a warrior princess. She was a beautiful and virginal maiden. Surely, she would save me.

At the very top of the tapestry is a cerulean sky that has never seen smokestacks. The air was clean then. The forests were new, the land almost untouched by human hands and machines that were yet to be invented. The mountains smiled upon us. Everyone believed that I existed. It was undeniable that the earth was as alive as you or I. I could see the breath of trees – the vibration of everything.

I was found and captured – my story stitched into the warp and weft of centuries. Most of the threads are common and natural such as linen and cotton. But some of the threads are metallic. The glitter is magic – not only the stuff of my life but of yours too. These are the years that led to yours.

There were so many javelins coming toward me that I couldn't stop to wonder then. But I do now. Who struck the final blow – if indeed there was one? Was it my human friend? I think of him as my friend, because he was the closest I've ever gotten to having a human friend. (I'll tell you about him later.) I'm not saying that I was above reproach. Perhaps no one is ever really innocent. Looking back on that day, I realized that many wanted me dead. But I did not understand why – or perhaps I should say I refused to. To tell you the truth, I never thought of myself as dying. I know it is inevitable, but perhaps I was too vain. I thought that what happened to all other beings wouldn't necessarily happen to me.

I found myself musing and arranging words that came tumbling out:

"You will find that I am the creature written about in holy books, and the one associated with evil.

You will find that I am the rareness that is everywhere.

I am many. I am one.

I desire to be alone – yet I am always with you.

Wise men have written that I cannot be taken alive. Others say I am dead.

Worse, others deny that I ever existed.

Why do you belittle me, when I am wiser than thought?

I am the revered and the scorned one

I am the one who is always seen and the invisible one.

I am your purity, your hallucinations run wild.

I am said to represent your salvation – with my one horn.

But I existed long before this was said.

My will extends further into the future than you can see.

I am in the clouds above you.

I am the darkness of the woods.

I was captured, but I am free.

I answer to no man.

Even as you deny me, I am you."

Chapter Two

It all started innocently enough. That's what I used to tell myself. Although when I think back on it, I have a nagging doubt. Maybe it *wasn't* so innocent. I knew he was spying on me. I pretended that I did not see him behind the bush. Instead of running away, I slowly walked to the nearby pond, bent my head, and admired my reflection. I kicked up my heels and pranced. My kind is known to be vain. I am no exception.

I knew I was being watched. I knew it was the same one who was watching me. I never thought there was any harm in making him desire me. We were different species. I knew that nothing could happen between us. But I admit that I liked being admired.

That day in the clearing when I saw him gazing at me with intense desire, I felt powerful but, at the same time, had a sensation that felt like the earth was sinking and might soon open and swallow me. I see now that I knew then that it was the beginning of the end. I had wandered into the clearing quite by chance. I remembered that the sunlit grotto was edged with stands of birch trees. Their snow-white bark the same color as me, I usually hid behind them easily. But I wasn't thinking of hiding that day. If I was thinking at all, I was thinking about the grotto and how I loved sitting in it and basking in the sun.

When I looked up, I would see towering pines framing clear blue sky.

This clearing was my favorite place. I must have known that I was walking toward it. But at the time I really wasn't thinking about where I was going. I just ambled through the undergrowth of the forest – admiring the curling fronds of the ferns. When I arrived in the clearing, I kept walking until I felt the sun shining down on my shoulders and haunches. I knelt down in the middle, with my front legs extended so that I was resting on my hooves. Then I relaxed. I closed my eyes and felt the sun's rays warm my outsides and enter my insides too. For a moment I felt totally free – as if I were made of sunlight. Then I sniffed and caught a human scent. I opened my eyes and saw him gazing at me.

I should have fled. I would have ordinarily. Maybe I needed to prove to myself that it was my right to sit in the sun and shimmer – no matter what. But now that I think about it, I admit that his desire made me feel powerful. He gazed at me with such awe that I could feel it. It felt as if I symbolized something in his mind – like the light of creation.

Maybe in that moment, I *was* the light that haloed me. But the light falls on us all and emanates from us all. He did not desire anything in me that he couldn't have found in himself.

I should have stayed outside the abbey walls that day and gone to the land near the castle like I had been planning. A stand of interesting rushes grew near the moat. They had long brown seed pods that were very tasty. I was always very cautious when I was near the castle, because this was the Middle Ages and barbarians in armor riding horses (who looked like they could be my cousins) and shooting flaming arrows could show up any time.

However, I almost never encountered anyone there on the land near the castle – except that one time when I ran into the princess and some other young women. They were jousting in the clearing. The tables were turned then. I was the one spying on them. The princess looked beautiful. Her dark blond hair flowed like a waterfall over the shoulders of her leather tunic. She wielded her javelin and her shield so well – like a muscular wind – that I barely noticed the other young women. I could tell that she would become a great warrior princess, one descended from the Celtic warrior queens – perhaps from Boudica herself.

I learned about the great warrior queen by listening to the virginal maidens living deep in the forest. These maidens grew up to become the wild women who rode me naked, before they aged into wizened old witches. It did not matter that we were different species. When we connected, our eyes and hearts spoke a common language.

I had lain my head on the princess's lap a while back when she was a younger maiden. I vowed that one day I would do it again. I could tell by her sweet scent that she was still virginal – untouched by man. Even though she was becoming a fierce warrior, I had no fear of her. It was known that warrior princesses always use their powers for good. Like me, they can immediately sense the difference between good and evil. Plus, I had heard that she held the key to the King's heart. Her wish was his command.

But I did not go the castle grounds that day. Instead, I was drawn to my favorite clearing where I sat in the middle. In a moment or two, I sensed the young man watching me. I last saw him several years ago when he was a lad. Even then, there was something different about him. He hadn't stared like the others who treated me like some exotic object – like a fairy or an elf, something from a long-gone era. He simply looked at me then like he was gazing in still water and admiring himself. His look was one of recognition. Even then I was rare. Like the rest of my kind, I desired to be alone. But even though I was not often among humans, I saw everything that was going on. I remember that I felt like light, a bolt of energy that can be interpreted as lightning. I felt like the air that everyone breathes – including the trees. I sensed that I coexisted with the cosmos, holding everything together.

When this young man was a lad, he looked at me like he knew my secret and as if he knew his own secret as well. Perhaps it is true that everyone – plant, animal and human – holds the world together with their goodness.

I was following goodness that day which started in the morning with me putting my horn in the stream to purify the water so that the other creatures could drink. But some might say that I was, perhaps, too concerned with myself. When I bent my head down so that I could purify the stream, I gazed dreamily into my own reflection.

By the time I basked in the warm sunlight cascading down into the clearing, I knew I was being watched. I have always known I am beautiful. It's not a knowing really. It's a feeling. Even before I had ever seen a reflection of myself, I felt beautiful. Truth be told, I have never not felt beautiful. My beauty may come from spending so much time alone. I am complete within myself. This day was not the first time I felt a ring of light surrounding me, but this ring was particularly strong. When I looked at the young man staring at me, I let my gaze linger – perhaps a little too long.

I saw that his left eye was still larger than the right. It was so much larger that his two eyes looked like they belonged on two different human faces. Much time had passed. He had grown into a well-proportioned young man. Even though he was wearing the full-length brown robe with long sleeves and the hood that I saw so many of the human's wearing around here, I could tell – by the way the fabric draped under his rope belt – that he was strong and muscular. Brown fuzz crept across and above his upper lip. I could see his large toes at the edge of his sandals, peeking from the bottom of his robe.

He was standing there with awe on his face. I could see his grace. For a moment, as we stood there exchanging a look, he was radiant. Light pulsed around him. It was gone in an instant. But there was still a yellow aura around him. Suddenly, green tinged his aura as it shifted to the glow of desire and obsession. If I believed in human deities, I would say that Satan overtook him and corrupted something that was pure and made it evil.

This young man wanted to possess me – at least in that moment – in a way that was never possible. After all, we were two different species. Even if he were the same species as me, I would have no need for him. If I spent my time with another, rather than being alone – I would lose my beauty. Perhaps that is why my kind desired to be alone. If too many people saw us, our beauty might be stripped away. That is the difference between a radiant princess and an old whore. But who among us doesn't like being desired?

Later, I wondered if things would have been different if I had turned away. In hindsight, I thought that the young man desired me because I embodied everything he wanted. I was beyond peaceful. I was serene. I was content with myself. I see now that that is rare.

I was intoxicated – not with fermented pomegranates – but with the shimmer of being desired.

I broke our gaze – but I could feel that his eyes were still on me. I closed my eyes and willed myself to grow more radiant.

I felt the glow around me as I stood, kicked up my heels and pranced. I still remember how shafts of light parted the clouds and shone down as if from another world. Looking back, I realize that I felt powerful and alone in that shaft of light.

I told myself for a long time that it wasn't my fault. I just happened to be in the clearing when I sensed someone watching me. That was true. But I liked being watched. The desire of the young man fueled me. I wanted to be wanted.

I concluded that I may have willed myself to go to the clearing that day, because secretly – unbeknownst even to my-self – I wanted to disappear. It is said that my kind goes away in times of strife. I saw plenty of violence in those days. There was man's inhumanity to man and certainly to women. There was man against nature. There was enough disease for the eons. Still, I loved the beauty of the land – the untouched blue sky. I loved the other creatures – especially my friend and equal – the lion. I even loved most of the people. It is my hope that my kind will return one day.

Then I tired of prancing. I think the young, robed man and I wandered off in different directions at the same time. Maybe we were both bored – of being watched and watching. I suspected that he also knew that nothing could come of the chance meeting of two different species. Like most beings, I was always thinking of myself. I didn't think that this young man had anything to offer me. No one did really. I had no re-alization then that this chance meeting would alter the course of my life.

I walked out of the clearing toward the sound of bird feet on branches. I could hear their feet slowly lifting off tree branches as they flew toward a new feeding ground. I could hear the sweep of their wings. I heard their bird calls. Their throaty calls told me more than the weight of their feathered bodies. They told me that the birds were flocking to the other side of the abbey near the convent where the nuns had just put down some new seeds in their garden.

I followed the sounds of the birds as they flew. A waft of air carried the spiced scent of the wild pink roses that grew near the convent. I heard water cascading on stone. I knew I was near my destination. The fountain was in the middle of the square of the arched pavilion where the nuns lived. I had to be cautious since I could be caught in the square. I could always gallop away, of course. But I couldn't fly over the clay-tiled roof like the birds. When I first came here, I would hear the beautiful voices of the nuns singing. But then the voices were silent.

That day, I saw a strange man in workman's garb outside the convent. I was hiding behind the shiny leaves of the medlar bush – poised to flee if the man came my way. I had not seen him before and had no desire to have a second human see me that day. But I could see them. A silent nun came out of a bolted door. She was bringing the man something to drink. Her plain girlish face stared out from the headpiece of a white habit.

The man took the cup and spoke: "Thank you, kind sister. For even though it is a mild day, my carpentry work is physically taxing. Your kindness in this cup of water is greatly appreciated."

The nun smiled back at him. Radiance transformed her ordinariness into beauty and holiness. Something about her was ethereal – like a band of light in the sky.

"I know you have taken the vow of silence," the man said. "But your smile is enough for me. It says more than a thousand sermons."

A wide smile lit up the nun's countenance.

The man smiled back. His eyes were bright points of light. He became luminous also.

The carpenter and the nun stood there smiling at each other. A giant golden glow surrounded them as if they were one being.

I've heard of this, but never before have I seen it firsthand. It is called love at first sight. Humans have claimed it exists for them. It has never been my experience, save for when I looked at my reflection. But I always knew it was my reflection and not another creature as beautiful as I.

When I saw the carpenter and the nun, I came to know that love at first sight really did exist.

But even as I stood in awe – hiding behind the bush – I couldn't help but feel a little superior.

I could attain this same glow all by myself.

Chapter Three

I remember that day like I remember no other. I had been a monk for several years – which meant I was still a new monk. I walked slowly along the East wall of the abbey trying to look contemplative. Spring was at its height – between Eastertide and May Day.

It was difficult not to smile and point – even though I was alone. The East wall is the part of the grounds that is the most overgrown with nature. Everything was so alive! Birds pulled worms from the ground. Leaves on tree branches whispered my name. New green shoots beckoned. Just because you have taken the vows of chastity doesn't mean you can control the body's urges. That morning I was one with nature – with the new shoots and the flowers that were about to bloom. I felt glorious – and truth be told a little sinful.

I decided to stop at the clearing because that is where I had the best view of the clouds. On such a beautiful day, surely, I would see white wisps taking on angelical shapes in the clear blue sky. I was walking as if I had ears on the soles of my sandals and could hear the fold of each green blade of grass. Before I knew it, I was at the opening of the clearing. Next to the opening, the sprawling oak tree was nearly three times as wide as my parents' house in the village where I grew up.

I remembered the opening into the clearing because I came here as a boy – before I ever dreamed that I would live in the abbey. I knew the abbey then only as a little gem nestled in the crown of Christendom. This is how the village Priest described it. I lived then in the forest next to the village with my mother and father. After I completed my chores around our little sagging house, I would go out exploring. One day I entered the grounds of the abbey – there was a gap in the wall; it was easy for a child to wriggle through – and I saw a most beautiful creature that I had never seen before. The creature was white, had a scraggly beard and, most remarkably, a long single horn that pointed from the middle of its forehead to the heavens. I learned later that the creature is rarely seen by man. But I didn't know that at the time. The creature did not move. His head was in silhouette, and he stared at me with one eye.

The creature looked just as I remembered him. Except for the horn, the creature had the head of a white horse, complete with a long white mane. He continued to stare at me with his dark eye on the side of his head. I swear he winked as if to say, "I see you and it's all right." I felt at one with the creature. He emitted a calmness and serenity that filled me. I remember that I left more quietly than I had come. But that was long ago when I was a boy and still believed in magical creatures.

For a long time, I longed to see the creature again. Then I had a discussion with my village Priest. The Priest patted me on the head and said what I saw that day was not an actual creature – but a symbol from God of his only begotten son. The Priest started talking about how God's only begotten son represented two legs of the trinity. He said something about the Holy Ghost and eternal salvation meaning life ever after. I couldn't follow. But I did understand when he told me that I had a pure heart and should devote myself to God.

I began to daydream. I'm an only child and a son, too, so what the Priest said already applied to me. I figured that I didn't have to listen. Being an only child, I have spent much time alone and have a vivid imagination. Sometimes I think the things I imagine are real. It made sense to me that I would see things that others didn't. My parents named me Apolo after the sun God, although my name is spelled differently. This is another indication that I would see things differently – because I am unique. Also, it gives me a direct connection with God. I said that once to Mother. She told me to be careful what I said because it could be interpreted as blasphemy. Then she said that I should always be humble, because it says so in the Bible.

After I spoke to the Priest, I never expected to see the magical creature again. I didn't until I was a young monk. After I spoke to the village Priest, I decided to dedicate myself to God. My mother was elated. I could tell that she tried to subdue herself in the presence of my father. My father was a blacksmith and a man of few words. At first, he objected. He said that being a monk was no way for a man to earn a living. He said that his father had been a blacksmith and his father before him. When he had a son, he expected to pass the trade onto me and that I, in turn, would pass it on to my son. My mother spoke up for me. She told my father how pure of heart I was – too pure to become a blacksmith. She told him that I would live a protected life in the abbey. She told him that by me becoming a monk, it would bring blessings on the family. Finally, he saw how happy it made my mother that I had announced that I would devote myself to God. He said gruffly that it was a good way for me to learn how to read and write Latin since he couldn't afford to send me to one of new universities.

So that is how I came to dedicate myself to God and become a monk. But I continued to think of the beautiful creature. Would I ever see him again? The village Priest had said he was just a symbol. But I had seen him with his one gleaming horn. I longed to see him again. I believed I would. I knew the unicorn was real. I believed with an intensity that I hadn't felt since I was a boy. This was after my mother told me the stories that at first had made me laugh. Whoever heard of a sword being pulled from a stone – or a lady in a lake? But she told me the stories again and again, and I came to believe. In no time, it seemed, I was fervent.

During that time my mother would tell me the stories every night and insist that they were true. Her sea-green eyes bore into mine as she told me that I would make the stories even more true by believing. I believed in the stories. Eventually, I believed I would see my unicorn again. My belief invoked a magical sword being pulled from a stone, the lady of the lake who chose the fate of kings and a gleaming chalice held on high.

I believed that day when I was wandering the abbey grounds. I was near the eastern wall when I came to the clearing next to the wide-limbed oak with its many branches and its shiny dark leaves that resembled green mittens on a mystical man. I turned left under the oak tree's canopy of leaves and stood under the unusually wide horizontal branch that marks the entrance of the clearing.

What I saw took my breath away. It was the creature again, sitting in the middle of the clearing. At first, he didn't seem to notice me. He just knelt there with his head erect and eyes closed. He appeared to be soaking in the rays of the sun which descended in vertical shafts between the clouds. The rays of the sun came down in such a way that made the sky look like it opened to reveal the heavens above. Light fell on his gleaming head, back and haunches. Sitting there in the light, the creature looked like he was praying – rather he looked like he was prayer.

I had never seen such serenity.

Then he sniffed, opened his eyes, and saw me. At first, his muscles tensed as if he was going to bolt. I willed myself to stay still. Monks meditate for hours each day. I am normally very calm. I was pleased to see that the creature sensed my stillness. He remained sitting. He just moved his front hooves so that he could jump up and move fast if he wanted to. He did not move his head. His eye – his head still in profile – stared at me. His straggly beard hung down, his ears stood erect, and between them his long single horn jutted. He looked at me with his brown eye set in his white horse-like head. His eye seemed to widen and deepen. Then it twinkled as if to say, *I remember you – from when you were a lad.*

I smiled back. Perhaps my eyes twinkled in recognition, for I had seen him before when I was small. And I was grateful that he had so altered the course of my life. I remembered what the Priest had said – that this creature wasn't real but was in fact a symbol of God and his only begotten son. Soon after that I learned that the horn is not only magical – it is a symbol of the salvation that comes from the father and the son.

But the creature before me seemed real. He didn't seem like a symbol. Would a symbol have a twinkle in his deep brown eye?

I stood still – nary moving a muscle.

The birds sitting in the trees sung more sweetly. Breezes caressed me. Leaf rustled against leaf. Music was everywhere.

I felt mesmerized – as if entranced by an age-old elf or fairy.

Still keeping its eye on me, the creature rose. With shafts of light shining down on him, he began to prance around the clearing in short circles. Then he cantered in place.

The creature's body was tautness in motion. He seemed to be made of light.

I looked down and saw the outline of erect nipples in the short white fur that sloped down to the creature's underside.

Then I felt myself stirring under my robe. The creature in the clearing wasn't the only thing stiffening.

I decided that the creature must be female. There were rumors afloat about certain monks and priests being sodomites. I wasn't one of them. I didn't fantasize about men – or women – for that matter. My manhood had become hard several times – but only in nature when the beauty of the new shoots and the buds about to burst open spoke to me.

I must admit that I felt chivalry toward my unicorn as if I were a knight winning a tournament for my lady. But everyone knew that was pure – and I did not take my imaginings any further.

It seemed that this beautiful creature in front of me was speaking to me. She had to be real.

Suddenly, I realized that I desired her. I didn't desire her sexually, but my desire was heightened by my sudden awareness of my body. Did I desire her serenity for myself? Did I desire this so badly, I had to disturb her serenity to gain it for myself? Was that the only way I could be content now myself? Did seeing that much contentment in the creature make me agitated?

Did a strange energy settle over this beautiful creature? Was the energy Satan? Did he put her in my path to test me? All I knew was that I desired this magical creature with an intensity that I had never felt before.

Everything changed that day.

The creature wandered off. I felt compelled to follow. But the unicorn was swifter. Soon she was nowhere in sight.

A knight on horseback wandered into my path. I was about to duck for cover. But I was curious – for it is unheard of for knights to come into abbey grounds. But I was alert. Usually, wherever a knight is, his army is not far behind.

"Hail, young monk," he said, greeting me. "Do not be afraid. I come in peace – but I am seeking something."

I immediately felt protective of my unicorn.

"I regret that I cannot help you, because I have not seen anything out of the ordinary on this fine day," I quickly replied. I was nervous. I worried that I might have spoken too quickly. But the knight didn't seem to notice.

His suit of metal looked extremely old and ragged. The chain mail protecting his neck looked like it had been found in a woodpile. It was so dirty that I wouldn't have been surprised if I saw moss growing out of it.

When he pulled up the reins on the mottled gray and white horse his suit of armor creaked. The armor must have been rusty.

"That's okay," he said. He slurred his words. "Maybe you can help me. I'm searching for the Holy Grail, so I'll have a grand tale to tell at King Arthur's round table. It helps to while away the time to tell a story when you're drinking a pint or two – or three or four," he added with a grin.

He seemed to me to be the kind of "knight" – if indeed he was a knight – who spent his days at the ale house telling tales of days gone by.

I didn't have the heart to tell him that he was about a thousand years too late. Again, I recalled my mother telling me the tales of King Arthur when I was a lad. I remembered the story of King Arthur's wife, Queen Guinevere. She was known for her love affair with the King's lead knight, Sir Lancelot. My mother told me that this was a tale about the romantic independence of Welsh women.

I also remember my mother telling me about King Arthur's half-sister Morgan le Fay, an enchantress, sorceress and sworn enemy of King Arthur and the Knights of his Round Table. She had a special enmity for Lancelot because he did not return her love. Morgan le Fay lived on the Isle of Apples where King Arthur had been taken to recuperate from battle. When I became a monk, I learned that the Isle of Apples, also known as Avalon, was associated with the Glastonbury Abbey monks who just several centuries ago made their homes on this same land where they unearthed the bones of King Arthur and Queen Guinevere.

I told the so-called knight that the Holy Grail was probably in the castle far in the distance and pointed in the opposite direction from where my unicorn had gone. The knight looked doubtful.

But then I added, "where else would a magic vessel be other than in a fine home that could afford it?"

The knight nodded and took off in the direction of the castle. I doubted that he would make it any further than the nearest ale house – outside the abbey walls, of course.

I purposely pointed him in the opposite direction of the unicorn because I had suddenly decided that she was mine. She was my Holy Grail.

I quickly walked in the direction of the East wall of the abbey where the convent is. I frequently go there for solitude, because the nuns are cloistered and have taken a vow of silence.

I did not find my unicorn.

But I did come across a young nun gazing radiantly at a carpenter. When I peered closer, I saw that he was drinking from a cup.

I was silent and stayed behind a cluster of trees, as I watched the nun's shining face. She smiled at him. The look between them was so beautiful that I stood and watched from my hiding spot.

When the carpenter had taken his last sip, he swallowed and said, "I am but a simple carpenter and I know you are a nun, but I love you. If you promise to come away with me, I will build a house for us and provide for you always."

I knew that I was on the verge of witnessing blasphemy. The nun might forsake her vows. She was in danger of betraying God and his son, the savior. I should have reported this to someone, but I couldn't move. I was transfixed by their love. This man felt the same way about the nun as I did about the unicorn. But they were the same species and could spend their lives together.

The nun was smiling and nodded. She seemed to have stars in her eyes.

They were each haloed with a golden light that united them. I knew that in the Church's eyes, this was wrong. But I could see that what they felt for each other was holy.

Chapter Four

"What do you mean when you say that 'God is love?' I don't understand," I replied.

It was late in the afternoon after my Latin class – which the Priest taught – and I was in his office in the church adjacent to the sanctuary. He was behind his desk, nearly hidden by stacks of thick books covered in thick parchment. Next to the books, scrolls were piled high.

A quill pen in a stand sat on the front of his desk next to a clay jar with dark splashes on the sides. In the middle of the desk, three unlit tapered candles stood on a pounded metal candlestick. It would be several hours at least before the Priest had to light the candles. The new monks customarily met weekly with a teacher. Since Latin was such an important topic, I chose Father Matthew even though he was a bit prickly. A perpetual sadness tempered his irritability. His sunken eyes looked haunted. The corners of his eyes turned down at the outside. He always looked sad – as if he had seen a great many losses and expected more.

The wall behind his desk was filled with tall shelves that housed slanting books and were filled with piles of scrolls. Nooks and crannies were everywhere. At the top of the towering shelf – close to the ceiling – a skull grimaced down.

If I had gone back in time a thousand years, this might have been a sorcerer's study – instead of a priest's office.

"I am quoting from the Bible— specifically from the Gospel According to John," snapped the Priest with a note of sadness in his voice. "God cannot be God without love, 'because God is love.'" He paused and looked at me. I saw that that the wispy brown hair on his head was thinning as apparently was his patience. "This should sound familiar. I read it in class last week."

I had a dim recollection of him reading this in Latin when he stopped writing and tapped his pointer on the board at the words: *Deus caritas est.* I had been daydreaming, no doubt along with the other monks and young men studying for the priesthood. It was a warm morning and we were taking a break from learning the conjugation of Latin verbs.

I wanted to learn Latin. The monastery taught us that it was the language of the world – the important places in the world.

But our lesson – active, passive voice combined with passive but active meaning and defective verbs – wearied me. I was willing to stick with my Northern influenced dialect of Middle French, but the teacher had told us with great authority that Latin was the language of religious contemplation.

That we had been taking a break from conjugating Latin verbs by learning the Bible, did nothing to alleviate the heaviness of my eyelids. I had suspected that most of the other young men in the classroom shared my sentiments.

"'Whoever does not love does not know God, because God is love, because God is love,'" repeated the Priest. As he sat behind his massive desk in the dim room, pinpoints of light came from his eyes. Behind him, light filtered down from high rectangular windows. He spoke methodically. "This is from the First Epistle of John."

Then I remembered. His words prompted me to think of the magical creature I had seen. I *did* understand love. Therefore, I understood God. I was so excited that the words burst out of my mouth.

"Father – excuse me" – I remembered my manners at the last minute – "I thought at first that I didn't understand. I thought the verse you read didn't make sense to me, because I renounced my worldly claim to love when I took vows to become a monk. But just the other day, I came across a magical creature in the abbey. I saw her once before – maybe it was the same one – when I was a lad. I didn't understand then that the sighting was so rare. This time when I saw her, I was again flooded with love. So – I *do* understand."

"It is hardly the same to compare a mythical creature with the Bible." Father Matthew picked a book and thumped it on his desk. I assumed that the tome was the New Testament.

"I didn't say she was a mythical creature," I countered. "I said that she is a magical creature. She's real. I've read about her in books. She's called a unicorn – a 'uni-hyphen-corn' – meaning one horn in Latin."

The Priest glowered at me. He was in his natural state – a mixture of piety and anger mixed with great sadness. My revelation seemed to heighten this.

"I refuse to believe that such a thing exists," he stated.

"But Father, I saw her with my own two eyes," I replied. "And I read about her kind in the Bible and in the bestiaries that were passed down from the Greeks."

"The Bible! I never heard of unicorns being mentioned," the Priest scoffed.

"There are numerous references, but my favorite is from the Psalms Chapter 92. Verse 10 reads, 'But my horn shalt thou exalt like *the horn of* an unicorn: I shall be anointed with fresh oil,'" I recited.

"Ohhh – the Old Testament." The Priest waved his hand dismissively.

He didn't seem impressed that I had memorized the verses.

"There are numerous references, Father. Another is from Numbers 24: 8. 'God brought him forth out of Egypt; he hath as it were the strength of an unicorn: he shall eat up the nations his enemies, and shall break their bones, and pierce *them* through with his arrows.'"

"But that is from the Old Testament, too. I doubt there are any mentions of the beast in the New Testament," said the Priest sternly.

"No, Father," I admitted. I hung my head. Then I brightened. "But my mother used to tell me a story about a unicorn in the Bible. God asked Adam to name all the creatures of the land and Adam named the unicorn first. Then, the hand of God came down and touched the unicorn's horn. Surely, that was a sign that God believed in the unicorn."

"God believed in the unicorn?" The Priest looked amused. "I haven't heard that one before. It sounds like your mother was telling you an old folktale. Someone probably read about the animal in one of the bestiaries and then elaborated on the tale. You need to be careful about believing something like that."

"But father, unicorns are mentioned in the Bible."

"In the *Old* Testament. Leave it to the Jews to believe in unicorns," sneered the Priest derisively.

I straightened my posture in preparation to counter his words. Jews weren't so bad. None had lived in the village where I had grown up, but I had met several Jewish merchants passing through town when I was a lad. When I was older, I had heard that several Jews had come to the Sorbonne, the university in Paris that was constructed in the 1200s, to teach the history of religion.

I was just about to open my mouth to defend the Jews when I noticed that the Priest was looking at me with an odd gleam in his eye.

"I'm surprised that you took the time to actually read the Bible," he said. "Most new monks just look at illuminated manuscripts."

I beamed at the Priest and said, "I love to read Father." This was true, but I neglected to say that I loved looking at the pictures too. The books with the color illustrations were called "illuminated manuscripts" for a reason. The illustrations were beautiful and were painted by hand in bright colors. The reds were so bright they almost resembled the glowing embers in the center of flames. The deepest blue – which looked Persian – was almost sapphire. The gold highlights – which were so bright that they led me to believe they were painted with a mixture that included the actual metal – let in the light. I especially loved the illuminations with animals in them. They led me to reading the verses about the unicorn.

"That's good son," he replied. "Reading will get you far in life – *IF* you read the right things. Since Gutenberg, however, far too many people have been reading. Fortunately – or maybe it's unfortunately – most are reading romances to entertain themselves," he scoffed.

I looked at him quizzically. I didn't know how to respond. Was my Latin teacher really saying that people shouldn't read? I knew I should be silent, but I couldn't help from bursting into a question:

"But father, isn't it good that people read?"

"My son – here in the abbey, we always read the *right* texts," said Father Matthew.

I nodded.

"Read what I teach, and you will learn how to think and to know when to be silent," he stated.

I bristled. I was a monk. I knew the virtues of being silent. Silence let me be my true self and be free of myself at the same time. This allowed me to be a vessel for God. Being silent much of the time meant that I was more focused in my labors, which included gardening and feeding the animals. The farm animals were kept so that the abbey could feed the Priests. Their leftovers were saved for the monks and the other poor people.

"I am a Priest – so I will always be above you in the hierarchy of the church – unless you aspire to a greater station," said Father Matthew.

I said nothing. I did want to further myself, but I suspected that the Priest might resent this. I became a monk because my village Priest suggested it. But this was also the only way I could learn Latin. But I wanted to learn Greek also, so I could read the New Testament in the language it was written in. But it was more than my love of language that made me aspire to a greater station in life. I saw the way that the monks – and the nearby villagers – deferred to the Priest. I saw that they valued what he said. I wanted that.

But I said nothing.

The Priest regarded me in silence.

"Regardless of your aspirations, I strongly suggest that you not speak of such things as unicorns," he said lifting his eyebrows. "This beast belongs to the mythical past – along with witches and sorcerers."

"But..." the Priest looked at me keenly.

"What?" I asked.

"Oh, never mind. I was just thinking that if this creature did exist ... and if you proved it did exist by, say, helping others capture it, I'm sure the King – and the Bishop – maybe even the Arch Bishop – would make it worth your while. Ever since our beloved King Charles the Sixth failed in trying to trick the wild people in the woods into bringing him a unicorn, there has been a royal obsession with capturing a unicorn. If you can lead the King to a unicorn, it would cement your name into their minds.

I recoiled inwardly but remained silent. Yes, I wanted more authority. I wanted people to listen to me. But I felt that I could never betray my object of purity. I shuddered.

The Priest shrugged and said, "Have it your way then. What you speak of is called 'mysticism.' It is a thing of the past. If such creatures ever existed – and I doubt they did – their only purpose was to convert pagans to Christians."

"So, you admit that the unicorn is a symbol of Christianity. That is what my village Priest told me when I was a lad and I saw the beautiful creature the first time. He told me that I saw the creature because I had a pureness of heart. Then he suggested that I become a monk and live in the abbey."

The Priest softened in his reply: "You were right to take the advice of your village Priest."

I couldn't help interjecting: "But I saw her again, just the other day."

"Tell me, why do you keep referring to the beast as 'she'?

"Because my love for the unicorn is pure and I do not want anyone to think I am a sodo—"

Just then I heard the door to the hall creak open behind me. The other door, which led to the sanctuary, was in the back corner behind the Priest.

"Matthew…I mean Father, I need to see you," I recognized the unusually high and melodious voice as belonging to a monk who sat in the row ahead of me in Latin class and who sang in the choir.

"Not now, Gregory. But I can see you tonight, after vespers."

I watched the Priest watch Gregory walk away. The desire on my teacher's face, made me feel green with jealousy. It wasn't that I desired the Priest or even that I wanted him to desire me. But I knew that he would never want me in the way that it was obvious that he wanted Gregory. All I had to offer was my mind. But I knew with a sinking feeling that it would never be enough. I hadn't believed the rumors, but now there was no misunderstanding. He was a sodomite. The Priest parted his lips and licked them. He had an otherworldly and partly lascivious gaze on his face – as if he was transported by the monk's voice. He looked less sad. I detected a faint golden glow around the Priest – the same glow that I had seen around the nun and the carpenter. Finally, he snapped his gaze back on me.

Did this have something to do with the "God is love" verse the Priest had been quoting? If so, why was love between two men forbidden? It seemed that love was love. And, clearly, love was holy.

"You were telling me why you referred to the creature as 'she.' I was wondering... need I remind you that women are impure?" Almost everything is referred to as 'he' as a matter of fact."

"My intent toward the creature is pure. I am in awe of her, and she seems to me to be female. When I behold her, I understand love," I said and looked at the Priest expectantly. I finally understood what he had been trying to teach me. I thought he would be happy.

It's true that I was aroused when I saw the unicorn. But that was because I was in nature and there's nothing purer in nature than the unicorn. But I would no sooner think of defiling such a beautiful creature as I would think of taking the pristine mountaintops as a lover. I really wasn't attracted to men – or to women either for that matter. Perhaps I didn't have a sexuality – or perhaps I had my own kind of sexuality that suited me to the monkhood in more ways than one.

"That is good that you understand," the Priest replied softly. "But it still doesn't explain why you are referring to the beast as 'she.'"

Maybe the Priest was suspicious of my intention. When I was a lad, I had heard a few older boys joking around about another boy being alone with a sheep. Even if I could catch the unicorn, I would never dream of corrupting her in that way. And since I had only seen smoothness in the lines around her genitalia – not the bumpiness of male genitalia, I would always think of the unicorn as she.

"I think she is a she," I replied. "And since I love her so – with pure intention – I don't want anyone to think I am a sodom—"

"That doesn't matter," snapped the Priest. His eyes darted from side to side as if someone else was in the room watching us. "You should refer to the beast as a 'he' – as with all creatures. In this case it doesn't matter, since the beast doesn't exist. But remember what I told you – all women are impure."

I was resigned to the fact that he didn't understand about the unicorn. But his comment about all women being impure made me angry.

"But Father, my mother is not impure. Without her, I wouldn't be here."

The Priest looked at me oddly.

"It is natural," he said, "for you to be grateful to the one who bore you. But remember we all owe our existence to God the Father."

I bowed my head slightly. "Of course, I know that I owe my existence to God the Father. But my own father is a blacksmith. He expected me to follow in his footsteps. He wanted me to apprentice with him when I was seven. At first, he insisted that there was no reason for me to go to school first to learn to read and write. It was my mother who agreed with the village Priest that I should become a monk. My father saw that she was right and here I am.

"My mother has long been interested in religion," I added. "When I was a boy, she used to tell me about something called 'the Secret Gospels.'" I paused, sensing that I should be quiet – that my mother had called them "the Secret Gospels" for a reason. But I could not stop myself. "These gospels were forbidden by the Church because they contained the story of Jesus and Mary of Magdala. My mother told me that the Gospels were called 'Secret' because if it were true that Jesus and Mary of Magdala married and had children, then Jesus most likely didn't die on the cross. In fact, my mother said that she and many she knew did not honor the crucifix, because it represents torture and agony.

"These Gospels also say that Mary of Magdala was an important disciple. She may have been the most important disciple," I continued.

The more I talked, the more I sensed that I should not be telling this story to a priest – and perhaps not to this one in particular – but I was curious at what he had to say. I had to admit that I liked provoking him. I smiled smugly at him and all the while I was thinking – *so what do you have to say to that? You may think that you know everything, but you don't.*

"I have heard the stories – but the stories were called the 'Forbidden Gospels' not the 'Secret' ones." The Priest sneered dismissively when he said "Secret" as if he read my mind and was saying with his facial expression that he really did know everything.

"Either way, it is the same thing. I know all about Mary of Magdala and what I know is that she was a whore. She was never an important disciple to Jesus, and never anything close to an equal in his eyes. She was never even a wife. She was just a whore — like most women."

I sat there speechless just staring at him with wide eyes. Everything he had just said was a direct contradiction to what my mother had told me. Who was telling the truth – my mother or the Priest?

"But my mother," I sputtered, "told me that the story of Jesus and Mary Magdala made Christianity more interesting. She told me that the crusades to Jerusalem weren't really to spread the word about Christianity but to seek the proof that it was more interesting. She said that the proof was the origin of the search for the Holy Grail."

"What your mother told you was false," stated the Priest.

I must have looked as shocked as I felt, because the Priest softened.

"I'm not saying that your mother lied to you. Most likely she was just repeating what was told to her. Since she is a woman, naturally she would take the side of other women."

"But it's not only my mother who told me there was probably some truth to the story of Jesus and Mary of Magdala. When I first came to the abbey another monk told me that his mother had told him of 'the Secret Gospels' too. He went to the library and read that Thomas Aquinas gave Mary of Magdala the title of the 'apostle to the apostles' because she was that important."

"Thomas Aquinas never said any such thing," snapped the Priest. He said it like he personally was there and knew everything Aquinas ever said. I knew that this wasn't true because Aquinas lived nearly three hundred years ago. But then I felt a meanness rise in me. The Priest *was* old. Maybe he was around in the 1200s.

When the Priest asked me what this monk's name was, I insisted that I could not remember. But I could remember. In fact, I could never forget. He was a few years older than me and his name was Guiscard. He told me that his name in the Old Norse meant "wise" and "horror." True to his name, he came to a tragic end. One day he left the abbey and it was said that he got lost in the woods and was eaten by wild animals. I always wondered if what they told us was true. Perhaps bandits killed him or maybe he took his own life. Maybe I shouldn't be so grim. A sympathetic priest may have overheard Guiscard talking about the "Secret Gospels" and decided to send the monk back to his village rather than letting him stay in the abbey where his words could lead to him being branded as a heretic.

I was so shaken by his death that this was the last time I became close friends with another monk. I refused to tell the Priest his name because I didn't want the same fate that befell him to befall me.

I left my teacher's office feeling frustrated, but that evening when I went to vespers, I remembered what I loved about being a monk. The other monks sat in the side pews next to me. We were all huddled in our robes, since it was always chilly in the sanctuary except in the hottest months of the summer. It felt as if we were one. The feeling continued when we knelt in front of the Priest and took the sacrament into our open mouths. The choir sang the hymn *"Pange Lingua Gloriosi"* by Saint Thomas Aquinas. I knew enough Latin now to pick out more than a few words. But a feeling of awe transcended meaning. The repetition of the lines of the hymn, the vaulted ceiling of the church, the tones of the organ breathing through the pipes on the wall, the feeling of being one with my brothers, and taking the sacrament from the Priest brought forth a feeling of grace. A warm liquid feeling spread from my chest and throughout my body. I was connected to everything around me. I was part of the great mystery and the mystery was in me. But it wasn't the taking of Jesus's body that I was thinking about. The stained-glass panel of the Virgin, wearing blue, looking down humbly and piously at the holy child swaddled in her arms, did move me. It was close to sunset, but there was enough light for me to see her image and feel her presence. She hovered over me protectively. But as I opened my heart and mouth and took in the host — from the Priest who was my teacher — I was thinking of the unicorn. As this realization blazed in my mind, I tried to focus my mind on Jesus in his sainted place on the cross. I closed my eyes tight and tried to think of nothing else – but my Lord personified as a man. To no avail, the unicorn — with shafts of light coming down from the heavens — was my savior. This creature was pure. Rays of heavenly light poured through me.

I walked single file with the other monks back to my pew. Anyone who looked upon me would think I was filled with the light of Christ — but I had learned that the light that filled me, the light of the unicorn, came from a pagan spring. The unicorn looming in my mind was my crown of thorns. I was cursed.

When the service was over, I stayed in my pew — instead of filing out with the others. I bent my head and prayed as hard as I ever had prayed for an answer to my dilemma. Finally, I decided that I would go the Priest and ask him to do an exorcism on me. I had the right feelings, but they were fixated on the wrong object. Surely, he could help me. I looked around to make sure everyone else was gone from the sanctuary. I tiptoed to the altar, through the apse, and to the door on the right that I knew led to the Priest's office in the south transept. I stood in the dark hallway and was about to enter his office when I heard noises. There was a muffled moaning and suppressed groans. The Priest's office was lit by a single candle. There was just enough light so that I could make out that there was someone in the room. Then I remembered that Gregory – a monk a year older than me – was coming to see the Priest tonight after vespers. I should have left. But I was riveted to the floor. I watched in the dimness until my eyes adjusted. Gregory was bent over next to the desk and the Priest was behind him. I wondered if the Priest was still sad as he moved back and forth or if this was the only way he could stop feeling sad.

Their robes were pulled high and as I watched, I saw that the Priest was surrounded by a flicker of golden light. It surrounded only him – not Gregory.

It occurred to me that Gregory most likely wanted to further his station. The monks and priests in the abbey were always scheming to get ahead. This was something that Gregory could offer the Priest. Much more handsome than me, he had a beautiful voice. And even under our monk's robes, I could tell that he was more developed than I.

Even if I were so handsome as to be desired by the Priest, I could not imagine doing sexual things with anyone to further myself. But I did have one thing to offer. The unicorn was real, and I would prove it.

Chapter Five

Now as I look at the tapestry and reflect on the scene, I remember being aware of the hunting party. I did not think it
had anything to do with me. I do not remember my young
man being with the party – I would have recognized him in
his brown hooded robe with his unusual eyes – one larger than
the other, staring off in different directions.

I was behind a stand of trees, right outside the scope of
the tapestry. The birch trees were white – providing me with
good camouflage. I kept one eye on the group of hunters. My
other eye looked idly at the flowers in the opposite direction.
The hunting party consisted of young men in tunics and tights.
At first, I thought they were young maidens – they all had
longish hair – and the bottom of their colorful tunics looked
like short skirts. Two of the men had skirts striped red and blue.

They looked like many of the uniformed school girls who
pass through this room.

As I look at the tapestry, I see that two of the hunters wear
shorter white tunics with a red stripe running down from the
shoulder. Two others wear red tights. Two sport blue tights.
One has bare legs. Another has a short brown tunic over red
tights. Three sport feather plumes in their hats. The two in
white tunics wear plain caps with no plumes. I see that a man

in a white tunic is coming through the forest to join them. He is partially hiding behind the limbs of an oak. The oak tree has magical powers. Some say the powers are warlike. This makes me wonder – *is he the one?* Now that I am looking at this tapestry – one would assume for all eternity but who knows, time has a way of leaving ruins in its wake – I see more than I saw that day. This is because I have been looking at the scene longer.

I see now, for example, that the hunters have five hunting dogs with them – not four as I originally thought. Three of the men are holding long-handled javelins. I cannot tell if the man coming through the trees also has a javelin. I suspect that he does.

When I was hiding, I kept my eye on them so that I could avoid them – but I did not think that their gathering was about me. You wouldn't know it looking at this tapestry – for I am not in it. The only reason that this tapestry is at all interesting is that it is in my room. I have heard many passing through call this the "unicorn room." I must admit, the tapestries that do contain images of me are much more beautiful and interesting. This is the only one of my tapestries that does not contain an image of me.

At the time, I assumed that the hunters wanted an excuse to show off their finery to each other. In my mind, this is really the reason for hunting parties. I kept one eye on the hunters and the other was searching for a hazel nut or a pomegranate tree – or at least an elderberry.

Somewhat hungry, I was looking for something to snack on. But my hunger could have been sated by a pond or a clear puddle – still water where I could drink in my reflection.

As vain as I am, I am – at times – filled with extreme modesty. These are the times that I realize I am not that special.

Years ago, I met a wise old unicorn. At first, I was shy. Perhaps I was unwilling to give up my rareness by talking to another creature like me. But I was overcome with curiosity and we did talk. This creature told me that many like us existed in far-away lands. Some were so fierce that they scared off all foes – animal and human alike.

The wise old unicorn told me that there was a type of unicorn long ago in the far in the East – just like us but a deep shade of green – who was said to possess the secret of three languages. What humans don't know is that we can understand any language if it is spoken from the heart. Our kind was seen by more than a few explorers in a land called India. We were large there – as tall as a horse – with white bodies like mine but with dark red heads and deep blue eyes. There was a horn in the middle of the creature's forehead, of course. The horn was about a foot and a half in length. The tip of the horn is the color of fresh blood, and the bottom of the horn is black. The wise old unicorn told me that these unicorns were hunted for their horns which were made into drinking cups. All types of cures – especially as an antidote to poison and a cure for mortality – are attributed to our horns. But I suspect that the status of having a unicorn cup on the dining table kept the hunters in business.

We speculated that this species of unicorn could not survive long – being hunted for its horn.

The wise old unicorn then told me about another creature in India like us. This unicorn was larger – taller even than the average horse and thicker. The wise old unicorn told me that this creature had reddish hair all over its body and ran as swiftly as the wind. Like us, the unicorns from previous ages – no matter their size and color – desired to be left alone.

The wise old unicorn and I parted company quickly. He – at least I assume he was a he – was on his way to find others

like me to tell them that they are not alone. It makes a difference knowing that you are not alone even when you want to
be alone. It's enough to know that others like me exist. Then
I went quite contentedly to my solitary existence, secure in
the fact that others – like me – do not seek their reflections in
each other's eyes. We do not desire to be liked, to be constantly
seen, or to impress. When you spend enough time with yourself, you don't notice that you are alone. Instead you are more
attuned to the natural world around you – to the shape of
each cloud, to the rustle of one blade of grass against another.
I find that I am more attuned to myself also – and to the fact
that there is a universe inside of me. I am complete in myself
and need no other.

So, I wandered away from the hunting party that day –
keeping one eye and ear alert for the hunters in case I had to
hide again. But the other part of me was following some interesting weeds – some prickly sow thistles with yellow flowers;
small heart-shaped green leaves; the pink flowers of chickweed,
and the ragged leaves of fat hen that are quite tasty.

Then I kept wandering in the wooded area next to the
abbey wall – until I found a small pond. I dipped my horn
in it. I was not thirsty, but some creatures who were would
probably come by – maybe a rabbit thumping its white tail, a
red fox with small, keen eyes. Maybe a falcon would come who
was freed from a royal wrist and – who knows? – an insomniac
owl might stumble by.

I bent my head and made the water pure with my horn. I
could see the pond scum fading away. I looked deeply into the
reflection of my eyes. My reflection rippled. The pond seemed
to deepen. My image, too, seemed to deepen. The sky shone
blue from behind my head. I was mesmerized. Then suddenly,
I became bored. I had to move immediately. Despite that I had

eaten from the succulent weeds, I was still hungry. I wanted to graze in the garden near the convent near the East wall. I continued my journey.

As I walked, I stopped to look at a vine growing from the wall. The slender vine was cracking the stone. I started to take a closer look but lost interest when I heard human voices. I went forward and hid behind a bush. Two people spoke in low tones. They probably didn't want to be overhead – even by me. I moved forward a little so I could hear them. I took a chance that they would be preoccupied and not see me.

A man in a long brown robe was standing near one of the marble pillars next the convent.

A nun faced him. I could see fear yet certainty in her face. She looked familiar. I realized that I had seen her before.

"Please help me," she said plaintively. "It is almost supper-time and my sisters will be wondering where I am. They may try to find me."

The robed man was running his hand over the white marble columns. The columns had carvings of human beings in them. I had seen them before. The carvings seemed to be portraying something. In one section, there was a star shining down on a baby lying in a cradle filled with carved marble straw.

"Please don't ask me to go back there," the nun pleaded. "The sisters mean well but they would never understand that I am leaving to follow a man who I met once. They would think me naive and sinful."

"Don't worry," said the robed man. "I will help you. But you are right, the others won't understand – especially Mother Superior."

The man's voice wavered as he continued.

"If anyone comes – *especially* the Mother – just say that you were showing these Biblical scenes in the columns to me and were on the way back to the convent. You can tell them that I am a new monk and didn't understand that you couldn't talk to me – and that you didn't want to hurt my feelings. I just spoke to the carpenter. He is on the other side of the wall waiting for you," said the man.

"You spoke to him?" asked the nun.

She tilted her face up and it caught the light and shone. I could tell that the nun had a pure heart like me and that she was intent on spending the rest of her life with the carpenter I had seen earlier. He must have captured her heart.

"I must go to him," said the nun.

"I am here to help you," said the robed man. "Follow me. There is a crack in the wall nearby that you can slip through."

He turned. I saw that he was my young friend with one eye larger than the other.

My heart warmed to see him.

I wanted to help the young nun in her secret journey, so I surrounded her with light for a safe passage.

"The sisters will miss you," said my young man. "Although they will put on a public face of scandal, they will privately understand that you are doing the only thing you can – by following your heart."

Chapter Six

There I was hiding near the abbey's East wall where I had just watched my young man assist the young nun in finding the crevice in the wall that she could pass through to join her carpenter.

I was sad to see her go – but happy at the same time. Everyone should follow their hearts. I have always known true love when I have seen it – for it as pure as me. I remembered how the nun and carpenter glowed when they looked at each other.

The nun who escaped – with her luminescent oval face – was one of my favorites. Once, a few years ago, I smelled the sweet scent of a virginal maiden and approached her slowly. At first, she stood very still. I could tell she saw me by the light sparkling in her eyes. She started making hand gestures motioning me toward her. Then she dropped to her knees and sat back. Before you know it, my head was in her lap. I used to come by the convent after that just to rest my head in her lap. She would caress my brow and then drop her hand and stroke the tip of my chin just under my beard. I was in heaven. But when I looked for her again and found her, she shooed me away. I remember that right before she succeeded in sending me away, she told me that the Mother Super suspected something and might have us followed. Then the young nun said she didn't want the Mother Superior to find us because she was very officious and would report me to the Bishop.

The young nun must have been prescient – because as I see now it is likely that someone has seen me and reported me to the Bishop. I wonder – was it my young man friend who had seen me or some unknown human who had glimpsed me unbeknownst to me? The Bishop had probably ordered the hunting party to be gathered with the goal of bringing me to the King. But at the time, I still didn't think that the hunting party – or maybe I should say the fancy-dress party – that I had hidden from earlier that day had anything to do with me.

I was spending my day the way I spent all my days – in pursuit of goodness. While I suspected that the hunters and their hounds were up to no good, I had admired their outfits. Then I had grazed in the direction of the convent and put light around the young nun so that she could safely escape to be with her carpenter. Next, I was en route to the far side of the convent where a pomegranate grove grew.

First, I had to navigate my way through a thicket. A yellow finch sat on a thorny branch where it poured out song like golden honey toward the path that I was seeking. I was content in the knowledge that I would reach my destination. I was alert, ready to hide from most if not all humans. But I still had no idea that the men in tights that I had seen that morning were at that very moment trying to track me down. If I had known, I might have been scornful. It is well known that it is impossible to catch a unicorn. We are swift as we are stealthy. Plus, I've heard it said that some humans don't believe we exist. How can you catch that which does not exist? Sure, the men had javelins and dogs. But how were they to run in their tights and boxy shoes? Plus, it was known that domestic animals are coddled – even hunting dogs.

I passed a thicket. I was so excited to be in sight of the leafy pomegranate trees that I saw the succulent bright-yellow flowers of a sow's ear and kept on going. You see, I wasn't as hungry as I was thirsty. Suddenly, I had an idea. The last time I had been to the pomegranate grove, I had insisted on eating the ripe fruit from the tree. Now, as I approached the grove, I could see the bruised red orbs between the jagged green leaves. That was several weeks ago, and my thinking then was that I wanted to eat the ripest fruit that I could reach. I had even speared the ripest fruit – higher up than my upturned mouth could reach – with my horn and then shook it on the ground. I had been munching on my hard-won perfect fruit when I noticed that there were other fruits nearby that had dropped to the ground. They seemed to be more liquid than fleshy. I went over and gingerly sniffed one. I had to share the fruit with buzzing bees who apparently found the rotting pomegranates to be quite the delicacy. Finally, I found a fermented fruit that didn't have bees on it and sniffed it.

I was tired. My stressful day had started with me having to hide from the hunting party. Even though I hadn't thought the gathering had anything to do with me, hiding was still stressful. Then I had purified a small pond with my horn while I gazed at my reflection. And this was *before* I had surrounded my favorite young, beautiful nun with protective light so that she could flee the abbey and live with her beloved carpenter. To do this, I first had to overcome my thought that if she ever did come back – which I doubted – she most likely would not be a virginal maiden anymore and I wouldn't be interested in resting my head in her lap.

I really needed a drink.

I got the idea yesterday when I saw a few birds flying. They were flying in unusual patterns – not in arcs like they usually did or flitting from tree to tree. The birds were zigging and zagging like they were not only directionless but giddy. An old crow perched on the branch of an oak tree near me and cawed, "They're flying that way because they ate fermented elderberries and THEY'RE DRUNK! Did you ever hear of anything so ridiculous – a bunch of DRUNK SPARROWS?!"

Crows can never keep their mouths shut. They're always cawing and complaining about something or bragging that they can do it better than anyone else – bird, beast, or human. I've learned to take whatever they say with a grain of salt. But in this instance, I was glad the crow told me what was going on – even if it wasn't exactly accurate.

For one thing, I didn't think the birds were smaller than sparrows. They may have been finches. Whatever they were, they looked happy that they were freed from their usual flying patterns. Birds seem free because they fly. But if you observe them for a long period of time, you'll notice that they do the same things over and over. They pull up worms from the earth. They peck at seeds on the ground. It's all about eating – which they do constantly, regardless of what kind of bird they are. They fly in the patterns they were born to fly in. I know because often I identify birds by their flight patterns. But these birds, zigzagging randomly across the sky seemed happy – like they were actually free.

I didn't know what the word "drunk" meant – the word that came forth from the crow's thin lips. But I knew that I wanted to try to achieve this state. I'm no whiz at math, but I knew I was big and the birds I saw were small. I knew that I'd have to eat so many fermented elderberries that I might get a stomachache. Then I thought of the pomegranates on the ground. If I was very careful – and avoided the bees – they were all mine.

I stopped at a holly bush and looked both ways. Then I turned my head and looked to the front of me and at the same time to the rear. It is very convenient having eyes on both sides of my head. Seeing that the coast was clear, I galloped to the grove.

Fermented red gems burst in my mouth, filling me with sweetness and bitterness. I barely noticed when I swallowed the seeds.

I bowed my head and drank from a fermented fruit. There were no bees that day. Either it was too mild for them or perhaps they had already had their fill. Then I found another fruit split down the center, lowered my head, and drank.

To tell you the truth, I lost track of time as I went, greedily gulping, from one fruit to another. I stopped to think that my beard and mouth must be red and maybe my horn too because I had speared a couple of fallen pomegranates to see if they were ready. But what did it matter? I would wash the red out later. I spent all my time hiding. So, no one would know anyway. What did I care, what people thought?

I was sated. I had no doubt that I'd do this again. The fermented pomegranate nectar tasted like more. I would be back. But for now, I was content to look around me. Everything was more vibrant. The greens of the shrubbery were greener than ever. I hadn't noticed that there were so many shades of green – from vibrant spring green to dark olive. The yellows and oranges of the flowers were brighter. The pomegranate trees in the grove had gnarled little trunks that resembled crooked legs. I looked up and saw that each tree was haloed with golden light that pulsed before fading into the vast blue sky behind it.

The sky! It was bluer than blue. The wisps of clouds were so white that I trembled before them and knelt. At first, just my front legs were bent. Then, I crouched on all fours and rolled over. I wriggled around and scratched my back on the ground. Who said that I was supposed to be standing all the time and looking elegant? This was much more fun!

I looked up in the sky and saw a cloud that resembled me with a thick body, an erect head sitting on a thick neck, and a horn that shot straight up. Other wisps resembled me – or parts of me. I imagined that I was flying through the sky. It really felt like I was touching the clouds and the vast blueness was inside of me. I was spinning, spinning, and then came down into myself. Words tumbled from my mouth:

"I was sent forth from the power,
>*and I have come to those who reflect upon me,*
>*and I have been found among those who seek after me.*
Look upon me, you who reflect upon me,
>*and you hearers, hear me.*
>*You who are waiting for me, take me to yourselves.*
And do not banish me from your sight.
And do not make your voice hate me, nor your hearing.
>*Do not be ignorant of me anywhere or any time.*
>*Be on your guard!*
>*Do not be ignorant of me.*

For I am the first and the last.
I am the honored one and the scorned one.

. . .

I am the utterance of my name.

Why, you who hate me, do you love me,

and hate those who love me?
You who deny me, confess me,
         and you who confess me, deny me.
You who tell the truth about me, lie about me,
         and you who have lied about me, tell the truth about me.
You who know me, be ignorant of me,
         and those who have not known me, let them know me.

. . . .

I am the one whom you have reflected upon,
         and you have scorned me.
I am unlearned,
         and they learn from me.
I am the one that you have despised,
         and you reflect upon me.
I am the one whom you have hidden from,
         and you appear to me.
But whenever you hide yourselves,
         I myself will appear.
For whenever you appear,
         I myself will hide from you.'"

I had no idea where the words had come from. Had I heard them somewhere? Were they stored in the ancient part of my mind? I knew that the words were as ancient as they were true.

Suddenly I realized that I was writhing around on the ground, saying words that rang true – but who knew what I looked like – or what I sounded like? I had put myself in a compromising position. Perhaps that is why my kind is always portrayed as standing and alert. Those who are different must be watchful.

I rolled over and assumed the standing position. I heard rustling ahead of me and I slowly went toward the sound. Perhaps I should say, I staggered toward the sound. Everything was still vibrant, but the ground underneath of me wasn't exactly where I thought it would be.

I poked my nose out of the grove, kept staggering and nearly fell into two women whispering on the far end of the convent – past the carved pillars. I backed up so they wouldn't see me – but I suspect they wouldn't have anyway. It was obvious they were entranced with each other.

"I love you," whispered the one standing closest to me.

"I love you too," replied the one with the deeper voice.

They kissed as if they were devouring each other – body and soul. A halo of golden light surrounded both them from the top of their habits to their sandaled toes beneath the hems of their white dresses.

Finally, they parted.

The one closest said, "If Mother Superior saw that, it would be the end of us."

And then the first giggled.

"It's not funny," whispered the one with the deeper voice, but then she giggled too.

"We're not even allowed to talk," replied the first one.

"There's a reason for that," said the one with the husky voice.

"Yes. We might have opinions," replied the other.

They both tittered.

I felt giddy too. Could it be that these nuns had drunk fermented pomegranate juice also? I recognized the nun nearest to me as one of the nuns whose lap I had lain in.

They both had the sweet scent of virgins.

How could it be that they loved each other so passionately – but they were still virginal maidens?

Chapter Seven

"The dactylic hexameter started in ancient Greece where it was used by the masters – starting with Homer when it was sung to an audience. Centuries later the dactylic hexameter began to be used by those who knew Latin. One example we have of a contemporary is Bernard of Cluny who lived right here in our Kingdom. Bernard was a monk at the monastery of Cluny in the Twelfth Century," lectured the teacher.

He was interrupted by a hand in the air.

"Yes, Thomas."

"But he's from the Twelfth Century – that was ages ago, Father. How can you call that contemporary?"

The teacher was silent. For a moment, he looked non-plussed – like this was something he hadn't thought about.

Thomas laughed, his melodic voice sounding like chimes. Abruptly, he asked, "In all seriousness though, Father – who were some of the early Latin writers who used the hexameter?"

I sat in the third row, next to Gregory. When I glanced in his direction, I saw him narrow his eyes at Thomas. Then his eyes widened. A new monk a year or so younger than Gregory, Thomas was startlingly handsome. He looked somewhat delicate with his big brown eyes, thick lashes, and curly dark locks. He frequently joked with the Father. I wondered if Gregory was worried about being replaced as the object of Father Matthew's affection. Younger and arguably more attractive than Gregory, Thomas also had a good rapport with the Father and possessed the ability to ask pertinent questions. I immediately felt superior because I had a plan for getting ahead that did NOT involve seducing the teacher. But I never thought that plan would bring any harm to my beloved unicorn. After all, the Priest didn't believe in her. How could you trap something that didn't exist?

"One of the earliest Latin writers to use hexameter was Virgil. The opening lines of the *Aeneid* are a classic example."

He recited the first ten lines or so in Latin. And then using his pointer tapped out the meter on his lectern: – "u u|– u u|– –|– – | – u u| – – "

"Amazing" commented Thomas, loud enough for the entire class to hear. "It really does sound like a horse galloping across the plains."

I recognized his melodic voice. He didn't bother to raise his hand this time. I looked over at Gregory. He nodded in Thomas's direction. I thought that Gregory would be threatened by Thomas. But could it be that Gregory was taken with him? Not only was Thomas good looking, but he seemed to be smart and wasn't modest about showing it. Gregory never made any comments during class. He seemed to be the type who relied on his good looks to get ahead. As soon as I had this thought, I felt ashamed. I shouldn't have thoughts like this about a brother monk. Still, I couldn't stop from smiling smugly.

Father Matthew pretended to ignore him. I say "pretended" because I sensed that the Father had noticed earlier that Gregory had narrowed his eyes in Thomas's direction. I guessed that the Father suspected Thomas was jealous. Even our teacher was human and enjoyed the rivalry. Father usually looked weary and sad when he taught. But now he brightened.

"Of course, the word hexameter comes from the Latin *hexa* – used to form compound phrases with the meaning of six, Father pontificated. "And the Latin *hexa* is from the Ancient Greek *hex* which means six. Hence when we say hexameter, what are we talking about?"

My hand shot up.

"Yes, Apolo?"

"Hexameter is a measure based on six feet or poetic meters. Each meter has two long or short stressed syllables in a row. Sometimes a foot is two short syllables – such as the opening of your line from Virgil. And it usually contains two dactyls which are each comprised of a long syllable, followed by two short syllables. A verse of hexameter ideally is six lines long and the last line is usually shorter than the rest," I said – maybe too eagerly.

Father Matthew nodded, but closed his eyes dismissively.

"The short answer to that would have been that 'hexameter' means six meters," he said.

A wave of titters rippled through the class. I felt like a fool.

Father didn't seem impressed. I wondered if I were being punished for knowing too much. I looked over at Gregory. He rolled his eyes as he exchanged a slight smirk with Father Matthew. Clearly, Gregory was not threatened by my knowledge. I realized, in fact, that his feeling toward me may well have been the opposite. He might have found me a bore for all the hours that I spent studying – while he relied on his good looks for the same grade or better. I had my own way of getting ahead. *I'll show him,* I thought.

Father Matthew tapped out the hexameter again.

"Of course, there are differences in how the meter of hexameter is used – particularly between Latin and Greek," said the teacher. "Since Latin *is* the superior language, we will focus on that. Virgil – perhaps as you could tell by my reading – used stronger and longer stressed syllables."

Father Matthew droned on about other ways in which the Latin hexameter was superior. But my mind wandered. I had already learned today's lesson through the reading that I had previously done on my own. The Priest's recitation of Virgil's Latin hexameters galloped through my mind. The pattern reminded me of something. I had an idea. I had found a Latin translation of *The Odyssey* in the abbey library and had memorized the first twenty lines. The rhythm was inside of me.

I would write my own epic in hexameter – in Latin of course. What better way to learn the lesson? Besides, my grasp of Latin had improved over the past few months —so much so that practicing the language had become a bit boring. I liked learning. Writing Latin in hexameter would make the language more interesting.

So, I began my hexameter in Latin:

I still / give thanks/ to God/ the father / who led / me with
His great/ might and light/ through the / forest of/ my youth
Where I / lived with / my lov /ing mother / and father /
in the peace
That gave/ me the / inner strength / and sil/ ence known/
as courage.
I had/ only/ been on/ the earth/ for fewer/ than ten/ years but
Could sense/ evil /from the good.

I prayed/ to God/ the father/ for protection /from beasts
With his/ wisdom/ he led/ me in/to the abbey/ where I

Slipped/ through a /dark crevice/ in the/mighty stone
wall/ and later
    The vill/age Priest/ told me/ this was /my destiny / this crack,
    To devote/ myself/, Apolo, with /my light/, my whole heart
    His light, God the father.

    I came/ to a/ clearing and/ peered in/ – there in / the sunlight
    Sat a/ creature/ that I/ had never/, before seen/ except
    In my /mind's eye/ as a lad/ at my/ fair mother's/ knee in
    Her bed/ time fair/y tales / the crea/ture came a/ live in
    My child/ mind as/ an em/blem of pur/ity and/ goodness
    Only/ I could see?

    The leaves/ of a/ tree in /the clearing/ dappled/ the light
    The ground/ beneath/ the leaves/ looked/ like lace/ on a
    Very/ fine maid/en's dress. /A knot/ in the/ tree trunk
    Seemed/ a face/ that was/ staring at/ me, express/ionless
    I pray/ed to/ God the/ Father/ to prot/ect me
    From magic.

    I stood/ still in/ this hallow/ed place/ and then was/ startled
    To see/ the creat/ure still/ there/ and looking/ at me:
    He resembled a small horse, except under his chin
    Hung a/ straggly/ beard, and/ from his/ forehead a long
straight horn
    I had/ never/ before/ seen such/ a creature, / but since/ I was
so young
    Did not/ know its rar/ity.

    The shin/ing white/ creature/ sat in/ a shaft of/ light
    So bright/ the light –/ illum/ination / could also have /
come from

Inside/ as if/ he were/ possess/ed with the/ pagan/
Titan Hel/ ios/ – not to/ be confus/ed with/ my name-
sake/ Apollo
Who, in/ later/ days of/ yore was/ known as/ the god
Of light/ and all things/ pagan.

This light/ had mag/ical/ powers. / I felt, / like Heli/os,
That I/ could see /and know/ all that was/ happening / on
earth.
Now I/ see mag/ic had / left me /feeling all/-powerful
As a/ pagan/ god – ev/en though/ I was still/a child.
I knew/ I should/ pray to/ God the / Father, to/ the One God
To rel/ ease me/ from this/ enchantment.

But the/ creature/ – who I/ now know/ as the un/icorn
Stared/ at me/ and with/ a twink/le in his/ eye spoke
To me/ and said:/ "You are/ pure at/ heart my lad/ I can
See this/ by the/ way you/ are in/cluded in/ my light.
I see/ a yel/low ha/ lo all a/round you/ – among
humans/ you are/ a de/light!"

Then as/ fast as/ the un/icorn/ appeared he
Vanish/ed – where/therein/ a gal/lop or flash/ of light –
I was/n't sure. / There was/ a cool/ snap in/ the air.
I long/ed for/ home and/ warmth and/ the love/ of my
Parents/ dear and/ so I/ prayed/ as hard/ as I/ could and as
If God/ the father heard

And with/ an invis/ible/ hand and/ guided me back/
through the
Crevice/ in the/ wall and/ unharmed/ I traversed /the forest
And re/turned/ to my/ mother dear/ to whom/ I told

This stor/y; she/ listen/ed – to/ her cred/it – without/ disbelief
And told/ me gently

That I/ must see/ the vil/lage Priest. / Father, I /began
And told/ him ev/erything. / He rep/lied that I /had seen
The son/ of God/ a sure/ sign that/ I must/ devote
Myself/ to the/ Father, / the one/ true light, my reason
For ever/ything. / Humble/ and pi/ous I came to the altar
Of my life.

I put my quill pen back into the ink well for the final
time and looked around. Class had ended. I must have been
so involved with my epic, I hadn't noticed that everyone –
except for me – had left. It was close to the end of the term.
Even monks become restless in the Spring. The room had
emptied. I could hear clatter in the hall. My fellow monks
and my teacher must have been oblivious to the fact that
they had left me behind. I told myself that it was just as
well. It was peaceful in here with everyone gone. I was stu-
dious and preferred solitude to the company of fellow monks
and aspiring priests – many whose families had paid handsomely for them to be here. I looked down at my epic still
on my desk. It told the story of how I had come to live in
the abbey – of why I had chosen to dedicate myself to God.
The poem would distinguish me from the rest. My fellow
students might be vying for power, but I had something
special. I would prove my story was true. I reread my poem
again, counting the syllables. I wasn't sure about including
a talking unicorn. I had made that part up. Maybe it was
a bit much. But Homer wrote that the gods and goddesses
spoke directly to King Ulysses about his journey. If people
believed in pagan gods in the ancient days, then maybe a

talking unicorn was believable. If it was good enough for Homer, it was good enough for me.

The footsteps in the hall subsided. I could hear voices nearby. Deep and authoritative, one sounded like Father Matthew demanding to see someone. The responding voice was melodious but petulant. It sounded like Gregory. Or was it Thomas?

Chapter Eight

The moments slid away. I sat in my chair across from the now familiar desk, piled with stacks of books and scrolls. Father Matthew hadn't yet arrived. His office seemed empty without him in it. Light fell through the high small window. I imagined the afternoon sun falling on the dial outside in the walled garden – shade from the larger triangle falling on the smaller notches.

It was two weeks after the term had ended. Before the last class, I had presented my epic to Father Matthew. He told me that it would be factored into my grade as extra credit. The grades had been posted. I received a "B." He hadn't yet commented on my poem. I was curious to hear what he said. Since my grade would have already been high, I wondered why I only received a "B" in the class.

Father Matthew was always punctual. He prided himself on being in his classroom when the first students arrived. For the past three months when I had been meeting with him in his office, he was already there when I arrived. Today was different.

In what was probably only a small amount of time but seemed like an eternity, the Priest arrived. He seemed flustered when he sat down. His hair – what there was of it – was disheveled. Wisps of thin brown hair went in different directions. A cowlick, on the top toward the back of his head, stuck straight up. His eyes were rimmed red. He looked sadder than usual – like he had been crying. Could it be?

He looked up at me briefly.

"I'm sorry I'm late," he mumbled. He seemed embarrassed.

He also seemed disappointed when he looked at me.

I wondered briefly if had just been with Gregory.

I'm the first to admit that I'm not much to look at. Having one eye bigger than the other, gives me a lopsided appearance. Plus, I'm underdeveloped – some would saw scrawny. And I'm shorter than most. Compared to gazing at Gregory – with his sandy blond hair, his square jaw and his broad shoulders – I'm sure looking at me *was* a disappointment.

But unlike Gregory, I knew how to use my mind. And I was here to expand it.

I was eager to talk about Saint Thomas of Aquinas whose hymn *"Pange Lingua Gloriosi"* I had been so swept away by at vespers. The next day I had gone to the abbey library and read about Saint Thomas of Aquinas. I learned that, in addition to writing hymns, he had been an Italian Priest and philosopher who had lived just a few centuries ago. Canonized as a Saint by Pope John XXII in 1323, he was the father of "Thomism." His basic theory was that good should replace evil. I was intrigued by his definition of love "to will the good of another."

Father Matthew shuffled through the papers and books on his desk. I decided to remind him I was there.

"I studied – on my own at the library – to learn about Saint Thomas of Aquinas," I prompted.

"St. Thomas Aquinas," retorted the Priest. "There's no 'of' – at least it's not commonly used," he said snidely.

I was taken aback by the Priest's obviously foul mood.

"Saint Thomas Aquinas," I replied after a moment. "I was captivated by his philosophy of goodness."

"It didn't come out of thin air," snapped the Priest. "Others have capitalized on the theme of so-called 'Goodness.'"

I looked at him blankly.

"Take Phillip the Good – you may have heard of him."

I continued to stare at him blankly.

"The Duke of Burgundy who lived in the last century," said the Priest with a sad, skeptical look on his face.

He looked like he thought it very tedious to be stuck talking to an ignoramus like me. But the fact was that my education here didn't stray far from religious topics.

"Actually, I'd be surprised if you *had* heard of him," said the Priest with a withering gaze. "If you had, you may have heard that he wasn't that *good* – according to his many mistresses who spoke badly about him.

He paused and must have realized how he was coming off – especially since we were discussing Aquinas's philosophy of goodness. I wondered if it had to do with the fact that he was carrying on with his students. Surely, that had ethical implications – in addition to the fact that he was a sodomite. Maybe the upper echelon didn't know, but I knew. More importantly: *God sees everything.*

"I mean … Aquinas is interesting, of course. But he was heavily influenced by Saint Augustine and that is where we are going to start," the Priest stated with his accustomed authority.

I gave him another blank look.

"I know our class on Christian philosophy doesn't begin until next term, but it's never too early to start learning."

I eagerly nodded.

"Augustine of Hippo was born in the third century and died in the fourth century. He was a bishop in the days when bishops had the authority of a Pope. He was also a preeminent Christian philosopher – one who helped develop Christianity."

I nodded again.

"He was canonized as a saint in 1303 by Pope Boniface VIII," said the Priest. His voice deepened as he lowered his pitch and spoke with great authority.

"Of course, like Aquinas, he was influenced by the philosophers – I should say the *pagan* philosophers. I am referring, of course, to Plato and Aristotle. Augustine may have learned from them, but he used their own tools to defeat them."

"How did he do that?"

"The ancients used stars, oracles, divination – all things pagan – to explain their world. Augustine taught us through reason that the scriptures can be looked at to refute all things pagan. Augustine was noted for his writings refuting paganism. In fact, he wrote many volumes on the subject."

"Then he must have been right," I replied.

"Of course, he was," snapped the Priest sounding more angry than sad.

I was his student – and my reply had been serious. But I had to admit that I suspected his motives in telling me this. He had called my unicorn pagan before, and I probably hadn't heard the last of it.

"That reminds me," the Priest commented, "I read your poem – and while you are to be commended for going beyond my assignments and giving me something for extra-credit, I found it fanciful."

"Fanciful?"

"Yes, fanciful – naive at best. That's why I reduced your grade to a B."

Shocked, I stared at him and opened my mouth to speak but nothing came out. I knew better than to contradict my teacher – a priest at that. But I couldn't fathom what I had just heard. I had given him an extra credit assignment and he *reduced* my grade?

"You are the authority, Father," I said and bowed my head. But in the next breath, I couldn't resist blurting, "But I demonstrated a working knowledge of the hexameter."

"A loose knowledge," replied the Priest.

"I counted the syllables," I insisted.

"Yes, but many of the stresses were different that the Latin approach that I was teaching."

"Yes, sir," I replied. I had temporarily regained control of myself, but I was thinking that *he* taught us that the form had been used loosely – as Bernard of Cluny had used it.

"I wrote the epic in Latin," I replied.

"It is expected that you have a basic command of Latin – especially as a third-year monk," the Priest crisply replied. "Besides, I wouldn't like to see you guilty of the Sin of Pride." His voice hit a note of finality.

"I should tell you that I have the poem in a special file here in my office. I wouldn't want it to get into the wrong hands. I suspect that some might declare that it is heresy to be so enamored of a beast – and a talking one?"

"I made that part up," I said petulantly.

"I'm relieved to hear you say that," replied the Priest. "At least I know that your mind hasn't left you entirely."

I nodded miserably. I had written my epic in hopes that it would help me.

"You write of one of the mythical beasts that is a pagan symbol. This makes you suspect for heresy, unless ..."

The Priest looked at me with a gleam in his eye.

"Unless what?"

"Unless you can prove that what you wrote is true – that you actually did meet the beast and you can prove that it is real."

"I told you that I can prove it," I countered.

"I hope so," said the Priest. "Or else I fear that all you will be known for is for writing fanciful poems and there are those who will consider – as Saint Augustine put it – that you have fallen into 'the sloth of ignorance.'"

I felt myself bristling but said nothing.

"Even if it does exist – the Bible states explicitly that man is superior to beast and that God made animals to serve man," he continued.

"Like women," I replied.

"Women?" The Priest blinked.

"The Bible states that God made woman – just like he made animals – to serve man," I answered.

"That's right," said the Priest. "Now you're getting it."

"But my mother – "

He interrupted by rolling his eyes and saying, "Yes, I know – your mother, your mother. Aren't you a little old for that?"

The Priest looked at me pointedly.

I returned his icy stare.

The Priest cleared his throat.

The reason we don't tolerate lesser gods," he stated, "is explained by Augustine when he says that basically the whole is greater than the parts. He makes clear that the one God – manifested through his son Jesus Christ and the Holy Ghost – makes the heavens more brilliant. He makes life endless. Multiple gods – which is paganism and heresy – can never be as great as the superior One God."

"The whole is called God," I responded.

"That's right," said the Priest approvingly. "Now you're getting it."

I smiled.

I *was* getting it. I really did want to learn what the Priest was teaching – even if he didn't like my epic. I became a monk because I wanted to devote myself to God. Ever since I can remember, I have always wanted to learn. I especially wanted to learn Latin – the language of empires. Now that I had learned Latin, I wanted to go further. I wanted people to listen to me, to seek my counsel like they did with the priests. I wanted the Bishop – and maybe even the King – to notice me. Maybe then I could rise in the ranks and become a priest. But I wanted to retain my purity. After all, it was the reason I had come to live in the abbey. But could I do both?

The Priest had a good point about the One God being more powerful. I wanted to believe. Certainly, I didn't want to suffer the fate of a heretic. I worried about my obsession with the unicorn. In my sheltered life, I hadn't had much experience with sin. But I had learned enough about sin that I was afraid that my obsession with the unicorn was interfering with my relationship with God. I thought about the night in vespers now some months ago, when I had felt as one with the other monks and when the hymns took me to an exalted place. I thought about the fact that it was the unicorn that I was thinking of – and not Jesus. I felt ashamed.

As if sensing my distress, the Priest looked at me with compassion and said, "Don't worry my son. We are all sinners."

I nodded and pretended that I knew what he was talking about.

"One of the things that Augustine is known for is his 'doctrine of love.' He wrote about forgiveness – which of course is related to love. In addition to forgiving others, it's important to forgive ourselves. In fact, some argue that you cannot forgive another without first forgiving yourself."

I smiled and nodded. This all made sense. No words were necessary from me.

"He also was the first to write about loving your neighbor as yourself. In saying this, he infers that it is first necessary to love yourself. When you truly love yourself, then you can love your neighbor and you can love God unconditionally," he stated.

The Priest was silent. So was I – for a moment.

Then my curiosity got the best of me and I asked, "What if you are ashamed of yourself – how can you find it in your heart to forgive yourself? And if you can't, how can you ever love your neighbor and how can you love God?"

The Priest looked at me oddly.

"That's a good question," he replied finally. "I do not know the answer. Perhaps I am not the best person to talk about love. I take the Christian writings seriously. I try to follow them. I follow my heart and each time it is a disaster. I love teaching and I love my students. But each term, things go too far, and I have my heart broken again," he cried.

I looked at him with sadness. He had his reasons for hating himself. Perhaps that's why he was snippy at times. How could he forgive himself, when the church told him he should be ashamed of himself?

This time I cleared my throat. I looked at him with tears in my eyes, and said, "Father – it is true that you know how to love, and it is true that you are worthy of love – from others, from God. I came to your office that night after vespers a few months ago. I saw you bent over the desk with Gregory – I saw the love that surrounded you."

The Priest looked at me as if he had seen a ghost.

"I don't know what —"

I looked at him gently and with compassion. I wasn't judging him. I was merely being honest.

He looked back at me and began to sob.

"So that was you. I sensed that someone was in my office besides me and Gregory that night," he said between gulps of air. "I've been so afraid. I thought it might have been another priest. I thought someone might try to blackmail me. I hope you will keep my secret."

I nodded gravely. Of course, I would keep his secret.

Now that the Priest had started talking, he couldn't stop.

"Now two weeks after the term ended, Gregory told me that he didn't want to see me anymore and that he was just interested in me because I could give him a good grade. He also told me that he is in love with another and doesn't want anyone else. I suspect it is Thomas."

I looked at him with compassion – but also with surprise. I was shocked that he was telling me this. It was a new level of honesty between us. He finally seemed human. I felt like I could ask the question that had been nagging at me for some time now.

"Father – if Jesus teaches us to love thy neighbor as ourselves, then why is it that people who don't believe what we do are burned at the stake? Are they not our neighbors? What is heresy all about?"

The Priest looked at me in wordless shock.

Chapter Nine

One morning I savored the small yellow flower nestled between the jagged green leaves of a sow's ear. The hunters were safely behind me. I still didn't think their gathering had anything to do with me. Perhaps hunters' gatherings never really have anything to do with the being they say they are hunting. It's likely the men were just using the group as an excuse to get together. They wanted to be in each other's company – so they told their wives that they were going out to hunt a stag or a fox. They made it sound manly. But I surmised it was just an excuse to dress in fancy clothes and impress each other. I could tell that they were hunters. Three of them were carrying javelins, including the two men with the plumed hats. They had hounds. But I thought they were hunting what they usually hunted, a stag or a fox.

I looked up from my flower and saw a stag nearby. His shining brown eyes elongated his face. The large dark holes of his shiny nostrils quivered.

Above his head were two long antlers. At first, I thought they were thick tree branches. His neck was long, thick, and straight, strong enough to hold up his majestic head.

I thought better of yelling to get his attention. It wasn't dignified. I spit out the remnants of the flower and approached the stag formally.

"Excuse me," I said.

The stag sniffed some small white blossoms on a holly bush. Absorbed in the smell, he did not seem to hear me at first. I did not blame him. I knew the holly blossoms were sweet.

I repeated myself.

"Are you talking to me?" The stag swung his majestic head in my direction.

I nodded.

Perhaps he was older than I thought and had hearing problems. I spoke loudly:

"I wanted to warn you – I spied a group of hunters nearby. It looks like they are organizing a hunting party. Probably, they are looking for someone like you.

The stag yawned.

"The men are dressed up – and they have javelins and hounds," I said.

"Hounds?"

I seemed to have gotten his attention.

"There are four of them on leashes. I suspect they will not be leashed for long," I conjectured.

"But they know who their masters are. Dogs will always be subservient to men." The stag sneered disdainfully as he spoke.

"That's true," I replied. "But it's also true that they can sniff us out."

"Yes," replied the stag. "But there are always men organizing a hunting party – or at least that's what they call it. It might be a party for them. But I can't be bothered," said the stag. His look of disdain changed to boredom.

"You say that now," I replied. "But later you will change your tune."

The stag turned a baleful eye on me.

"How do you know they aren't looking for *you*?" he asked – perhaps prophetically.

I looked back at him without blinking and said: "I avoid all men, even though I've heard that some deny my existence. Why would the hunting party be searching for something they might not find?"

"Why do they do anything?" asked the stag.

He was getting so ornery that I thought about turning my back. But I felt compelled to keep on talking.

"I'm just warning you," I replied.

The stag pawed the ground and snorted. He actually snorted.

"What kind of response is that?" I asked. "I was only trying to help."

"If you want to help, you can come and purify the stream near the fountain where the others are waiting."

"Others? What others?" I asked.

"The hyena, the lion, the hare – they are all gathered at the stream that I just came from," stated the stag.

"The lion?"

"I just told you. Yes, the lion – along with the others." The stag pawed the ground impatiently. "As you know, poisonous flowers grow on the banks of the stream."

I knew that, but I was determined not to be distracted.

"It is customary to put the lion first – not between the hyena and the hare," I insisted.

"Look. It is no concern of mine if you are friends with the lion. The hyena and the hare are just as important," insisted the stag.

"Really?" I asked. The stag seemed to be losing his patience.

"If you were a true friend to the lion, you'd go down to the stream and purify it so we all can drink."

Now it was my turn to turn a baleful eye on the stag. "I just purified the stream a few days ago. It still should be okay to drink from – even with the white campion flower growing there."

"But a serpent came by and spread his venom in the stream. The hyena saw him do it," countered the stag.

I shook my head. "Aaah – the serpent! If he's the same serpent I am thinking of, I've met him a few times. He's evil and cares only for himself."

"You can see why I need you to get over there right now." The stag sneered.

The stag's manner put me off. If he had asked me nicely, I would have gone right away.

But this was different.

I'll show him, I thought.

"Since I'm the only one who can purify the stream, you'll just have to wait until I get there," I replied serenely.

I turned away from the stag and began to walk slowly. I didn't know where I was going, but I did know that I had something to prove – *I did not take orders from him.*

Behind me, I heard the stag mutter, "I'll tell the others you are taking your good old time."

I refrained from turning my head and commenting. But I knew just what I would say if I didn't have manners – *you do that.*

The stag galloped ahead of me.

Finally – I was alone again. Despite my knowledge that the hunting party was somewhere nearby and despite the grumpiness of the stag, I felt suddenly peaceful – as if something in the universe had been decided. The abbey was a tranquil place. Men in robes walked about so quietly and sparsely that I rarely glimpsed anyone.

It's rare that I ran into hunting parties like I did earlier that morning. However, when I lived in the nearby forests with the villages nestled into them, it was quite common to spy hunting parties. That's one of the main reasons that I left and came to live here. There were too many people – gathering for festivals or hunting. It was all the same to me. They were too loud, even in their huts and tents. They made too much noise with their squalling children and their clatter.

By comparison, it was peaceful here.

I heard music coming from the chapel. Even that was serene. Whenever I heard the music, I never saw anyone walking around the grounds. I imagined all the people must be in the chapel. Perhaps they were learning to be silent. Maybe they were listening to the silence. It's possible that they were hearing their own inner voices for the first time. The music was so calm that even from a distance I felt its serenity. The music had pictures in it. I saw clouds billowing. I saw the rising sun casting its pink orange glow across the sky. I wondered if the images were same as the music. I was tempted to move closer to the chapel, to peer through the painted glass, but I didn't have to. I could find everything that I heard in the nature that was all around me.

A bird chirped. It was answered by another bird trilling a ripple of sound. The first bird chirped again. This time there were three chirps in a row. The birds must have been hiding in the trees because I could not see them. But I was attuned to their sounds. If bird sounds had shapes, they would look like their feet, like the strokes of an ancient language. Even though I couldn't see the birds – I could imagine them from the sounds that arced across the morning sky – still glowing with sunrise. I imagined that the highest chirps came from the smallest birds – full throated and full bellied even though they were small. The birds were not visible, but my imagination gave them colors. The small birds were yellow. The larger ones were blue and red. The ones in between were gray and brown, tinted pink and orange in the morning light.

Morning was my favorite time of the day. The soft, diffuse light let me look at the creatures around me with compassion. I even thought of the hounds this way – after all they were just doing their masters bidding. I can't imagine having a master. I looked upon the hunters with compassion, too. After all they were just doing what someone expected them to do. There was probably some human who was superior to them who ordered a hunting party and made it seem like it was an honor to serve him. I still cannot think of less of an honor than having to answer to someone. I was thankful that I have never had to serve anyone and for the fact that I never would have a master. I would rather die.

I found that being compassionate about others made me feel good about myself. Perhaps I was becoming more of myself. Usually, I would define myself by what I was not. I was not other creatures. I was not the stag (thank God!). I was not the lion. I was thankful to be me.

I never wanted to be male — like the hunters or even like my young robed friend. I didn't want to be female — like the nuns or even like the warrior princess. I was not the oak tree or the holly bush. I was not the fermented pomegranate fruits even though I liked to drink from them. I was not the hounds. I was not the chickens.

That morning – with sunrise flowing into forever and chirping birds sounding the bell of sky – I realized that I, by virtue of being myself, held the world together. I knew this when I gazed at tree tops and saw that they had a golden glow just above them. This was a pulsing field that breathed sky. The more I transcended myself, the more I became myself.

I have always recognized the good — and I have always known when to move away from the bad. That's why I moved away from the hunters and it was also why I turned away from the stag when it seemed he had nothing good to say and was inciting my ire.

Enticed by the clove-like fragrance of a nearby carnation, I stopped, lowered my head and inhaled. I breathed in again. The air was sweet. I inhaled again and held the sweetness deep in my belly before exhaling.

When I breathed in, everything around me became more still. When I breathed out, I heard the silence in the wind and then the birds as they began to chirp. Silence is rarely silent. In the void, I fell into a trance and was so delirious that I began to speak aloud:

"In the silence, I do not know my name.
And in the silence, I do not know that I have a name.
But I know myself in silence.
I exist in silence,
and I am myself in silence.
In the silence there is no difference between play and being.
In the silence, I don't have to pretend to be myself.
I am the silence.

I am I in the silence."

Then in the silence, I spoke words that I sensed were ancient and true:

"'I am the silence that is incomprehensible
    and the idea whose remembrance is frequent.
I am the voice whose sound is manifold
    and the word whose appearance is multiple'"

I looked up from the carnation and continued walking in the direction of the East wall of the abbey where the nuns lived. The fountain – that the stag had mentioned – was near the convent. I was taking my time. I was doing this so I wouldn't feel like I was obeying the stag by hurrying to purify the stream. I bent down to admire the bluebells. Nearby, the bistort thrust forth pink spikes above its deep green leaves.

Then I spied the convent gardens. The nuns were weeding in the rows of green shoots. I paused for a minute to look at their hindquarters clad in their habits. Since they were looking away from me, I didn't have to run and hide. I just walked fast until I had reached the medlar bush after the last pillar of the convent and hid behind it.

The same two women that I had seen before were standing together. But this time they were whispering to each other rather than kissing. I pointed my ears in their direction and listened.

"I think the Mother Superior suspects," whispered the one with the deeper voice. I noticed that she looked older than the other woman. Worry creased her forehead.

"Oh, you're imagining things," said the taller one. "Quick, give me a kiss."

"I am *not* imagining things," the shorter one replied. "The Mother narrowed her eyes at me when I said we were going out together to get water."

The shorter one leaned forward to furtively kiss her lover.

The taller one leaned down. They seemed suspended in time.

Then the moment passed.

I looked down. A wooden pail sat on the ground between the nuns.

"That's just because she frowns upon particular friend-ships," whispered the taller nun. "I'm sure she doesn't suspect anything else. Besides, I don't know why she should object."

"Why? Because it's against God's will, that's why." The nun with the deeper voice, spoke urgently.

"I don't understand," the taller one with the higher voice answered. "Jesus teaches us to love each other, and that's what we are doing. I didn't know that such a great love existed. You must feel the same way, don't you, Isabella?"

"Of course, I do Heloise. I love saying your name. Heloise, Heloise, Heloise. I love the feel of the word in my mouth – almost as much as I love having you in my mouth."

Heloise tittered and said, "It is a good thing that the Mother sleeps on the other side of the convent, or she might suspect something. We are quiet, but sometimes I fear that the other sisters might see us going into one another's rooms."

"Perhaps that is why our love is frowned upon," whispered Isabella. "Our love is so large that it is greater than our love of God."

"Nonsense," replied Heloise, looking down at her lover adoringly. "Our love is so great that it *is* God. It brings down heaven and puts it in our arms – that's how I feel when I hold you."

The two women started embracing and exchanged a long kiss. They sunk to the ground and knelt before lying next to one another. I sensed that I should turn away and I did. But as I turned, I inhaled deeply. The smell – of two virginal maidens – was as strong as it was sweet.

Chapter Ten

Now that I look at the tapestry, I wonder that I didn't know danger was right behind me.

My image is centered in the fabric – just under the fountain – kneeling with my front legs bent. My back legs are tucked under me also, but my hind quarters are higher. I had just lowered my head so that I could place my horn in the stream that runs in front of the fountain. I was cleansing the stream for my friends – the lion, the hyena, and the others. The stag was there too. I ignored him since we had words, but then I had almost forgotten what we were quarreling about. I remember that he just looked thirsty.

The distant castle where the warrior princes lived is behind us in the top left corner. If the little princess – the one who visited me earlier who spoke about there being "too much blood" – were here now and I could speak to her, I would tell her about the warrior princess who lived in the castle. But she is not here now, and when she was here, she was sobbing with memory so I could not speak to her. I want to tell her that everything will be okay – that the warrior princess will save me. Maybe I just want to make those reassurances to my younger self. Perhaps I just want my wishes to be true.

Far above the fountain in the middle of the tapestry –
toward the top left corner – I can see the distant castle. The
hunters are below that, standing in a semicircle above the fountain. They cannot see me because the tall marble fountain –
that has a basin below and tall tower in the middle, spitting out
streams of water through carved Gorgon masks – is between
us and protects me from their view. One of the hunters, with
a plume in his hat, is standing to the right of the fountain,
holding his finger straight up in the air. This man, with a red
and blue robe over his gold tunic, looks more important than
the others – or at least like he thinks of himself as important.
Perhaps he was telling the others to wait a minute. Maybe he
pretended that he knew the way. I suspect he was the organizer
of the exhibition. Someone probably convinced him that this
was an honor. The man standing behind him, on his right, has
his javelin thrown over his shoulder and has taken off his red
cap and holds it in his right hand. His long straight dirty blond
hair straggles down to just above his shoulders. His face is full.
His lips are turned down at the corners in the downtrodden
look of one who is used to carrying out orders. Below him, to
his right, two men are depicted as having a discussion. The one
on the left with the curly reddish blond hair and the bright red
cap looks at the man next to him with the darker red hat. The
man extends his arm as if he is making a point. Two hounds,
one white, one brown, are next to them. The dogs look up so
devotedly at their masters that it turns my stomach.

I see now that there is a dove, a pheasant and several small
birds perched high up above me on the edge of the fountain.
The pheasant has a blue neck on its red body. Its long gold
tail arcs over the fountain. The pheasant is busy drinking. But
the others – if they were really there – would have warned us
that the hunters were behind the fountain. I still didn't know

that the hunters were in pursuit of me. But if we had known that the hunters were there, all the animals would have left together and found another stream or pond. At the very least we would have scattered in different directions and met up later. The designer of the tapestry must have added the birds as an afterthought. I imagine most humans don't realize animals talk to each other.

Everywhere in the tapestry is green – at the top next to the castle and above the hunters are holly bushes with their tiny blossoms and red berries and hawthorn trees with their shiny green leaves and tiny white flowers. Next to them is the mighty oak with its green leaves of many fingers. Below the circle of hunters – around the fountain in the middle – are more trees, holly, hazelnut, and smaller oaks. There are also several medlar bushes, with their delectable small round orange fruits.

At the bottom, in front of the fountain, where I am kneeling and dipping my horn into the narrow stream, is a bed of sage (I remember that it was pungent) and next to that the broader and rounder leaves of clary with delicate purple flowers shooting up. Interspersed with the clary, is a ground cover of wild strawberry vines. On the opposite side of the stream, the animals sit and wait for me to finish purifying the water. On the left are the male and female lions, in the middle are several meerkats and at the far right is the hyena. The stag is opposite me, kneeling but alert, waiting for me to finish cleansing the water.

Looking at this scene, with the hunters in an arc above the fountain and me and the other wild creatures below the fountain, is like looking at good and evil. In the top part of the tapestry are the perpetrators of evil – the hunters and their hounds. My wild animal friends are with me under the fountain on the bottom. We are simply interested in quenching our

collective thirst with the goodness of the clear water that rip-
ples and forms the stream. But as I gaze at the tapestry — and
I have been gazing at it for a good many years – I must admit
there is more to it than that.

When I look at the man on the left, right behind me, who
is pointing in my direction, I see that he looks like my young
man friend who I saw in the clearing. Immediately, I remember
that time in the clearing. I am forced to admit that if I had
never enticed him, I wouldn't have been in this predicament.
Who knows? Maybe my kind would still be roaming the earth.

He looks different out of his robe. But I can tell from his
one large eye – his face is in silhouette – and from his well-kept
brown hair that comes to just below his ears, that it was him.
His hair, coming down from his red cap, is straight coming
down from the top for several inches and then forms ringlets.
A horn is slung over his shoulder – rather than a weapon. It
makes sense that he would be a guide and not a hunter. But
he is holding a hound on a short leash. The hound must have
sniffed me out. The others behind him have javelins, so he
must have known they were hunting me.

I remembered that day in the clearing. The sun was
shining down on me. I could feel myself shimmering. I just
happened to be there. For a long time, I told myself that I was
innocent, but was I really? When I slowly became aware that
he was watching me, I liked it.

I fed on his desire. It fueled me and filled me. In some
ways, I was no better than a village woman plying her wares
in a cemetery. I was aware that I could make him keep on
desiring me – and I did. I knew that the light that fell on
me made me appear to be something else. With the shafts of
sunlight warming my shoulders and my hindquarters – I felt
other worldly, ethereal. But I wasn't. I was flesh and blood like

everyone else. My bright white hue captured the light that was probably amplified by the birch trees. The young man's desire was a bolt of energy making me aware of my own beauty which intensified under his gaze. I knew that we were two different species. Nothing could come of a harmless flirtation. Right?

I certainly didn't want to hurt anyone – not the young man who I pranced for after I admired my reflection in the pond. I didn't want to hurt the birches or any of the trees, for that matter. They were all beautiful, each one of them. I didn't want to harm the ground under my feet or the sage plants or the clary that grew nearby. I did not want to harm the blades of grass under my hooves. And I certainly did not want to harm myself.

But did I think of any of that? No. I was so consumed in feeling all-powerful that I did not stop to think that my actions could hurt anyone or anything – or myself. I knew that the image I presented – whatever it was that the young man desired – was not me. It was the light falling on me in a certain way that cast me as other-worldly. I was unusual. But the fact is there were others like me. If my young man had lived earlier in another place — like in the East, in India — he would have known this. But even if I knew all this when I felt the energy of his obsession — would I have acknowledged it? Probably not. I was too preoccupied with my own reflection.

It is hard to admit that I most likely led to my own demise.

I was high-spirited then. I knew that I was beautiful, and I thought that nothing could touch me.

So, there I was. Innocently, I lowered my head and dipped my horn into the stream to cleanse the water for my thirsty friends. I had no idea what was to come.

Chapter Eleven

I left my cell early that morning, shortly after the church bell announced the day. Usually, I went to mass in the morning. But today was different. I wasn't planning on attending afternoon mass either. I would probably be back in time for vespers. Still, I felt guilty. But does God really care if I spend three hours on my knees praying each day? Doesn't God realize that I have better things to do? But as soon as I had the thought, I felt contrite. I wasn't that I had better things to do, but rather that I had *other* things to do. Time was passing quickly. In a few Sundays it would be the feast day of Pentecost.

I passed the kitchen – without sneaking in to get my morning bread – and walked by the storehouses. I heard grunts of the pigs in their pens. They were probably thinking I was coming to feed them. I could feel muscles bulging under my robe. I had become stronger since I started carrying buckets of water from the well for the pigs. This was usually my job when I didn't have the morning off. I heard a happy gurgling. There was a river flowing nearby that went through the abbey. I felt the smile of nature all around me. My mind wandered. It was rumored that the Bishop was going to build a mill. That would make it easier for the monks who ground the flour. No doubt, it would bring in revenue – not only from the abbey but from the nearby villages as well. The prices might be the same as other places, but at least the peasants would be assured that the miller who worked in the abbey was honest. God does see everything — including chalk dust mixed in with the flour. But I had also heard that the Bishop would recover his expenditure on the mill by requiring extra unpaid labor from the monks. It seemed like we could never win.

I had the morning off. I kept my eyes on the white wisps of clouds, tinted pink and orange, that streaked across the sky. I was excited because I planned to spend the day at the abbey library. The library was a large rectangular room in the outer corridor of the church. I had heard one of the other monks – or maybe he was a priest in training – say that he knew about other abbeys that had separate buildings for their libraries. It sounded like he thought it was a shame that he was here in this shabby abbey with monks who didn't know any better. It sounded like he thought that ignorance was the only reason that the monks were content. It made me angry that he didn't think that contentment with one's lot is a virtue. But I tried not to care what he thought. I was excited to go to the abbey library because it housed the eons. I rarely went, so it felt like a treat.

Just then I saw a hawk sweeping across the sky into the wisps of clouds. The sky was still tinted with the fading glow of the wash of the morning's pink and orange. The hawk's wingspan widened the sky into forever, wind-swept and vast. I came to a halt and stood reverently. It occurred to me that I was praying. I felt myself as part of the prayer of the hawk sweeping across the sky. I was awed by the presence of God more in nature than anywhere else. This included the chapel where I sat in silence and marveled at the patterns of the painted glass windows. I marveled at the windows in the morning and afternoon mass and at the evening vespers when the candlelight inside the church cast its flickering light on the shapes in the glass. I also was awed by the sacred sounds of the *"Pange Lingua"* by Saint Thomas Aquinas. This still was my favorite hymn and the most holy sounds that I have heard inside the church especially when it was played on the organ and accompanied by the angelic strings of the harpsichord.

I can see why it was chosen for the holy sacrament when we drank a small amount of wine and took the wafer that is Christ's body, into our mouths.

Every time I heard it, the music entered me. I felt my heart as a liquid center that spread through me and softened me to gentleness. When we ate our savior's flesh, we became one with Him — and therefore entered the kingdom of heaven. But that morning, as I watched the hawk soar across the sky, I felt the holiness more acutely. As I watched the creature, I soared into the Kingdom. The pink and orange tinted clouds moved through me. I was the vastness of the sky.

The mornings weren't always this quiet. A year or so ago, the nearby village beggars lined up daily at the church door asking for alms. The Bishop banned the beggars though, saying that they should stay in their village parishes. But the Bishop didn't ban the rich. On some Saturdays, the wedding parties of the more affluent families, who could pay the special price to be married in the abbey church, raised a ruckus. The funerals and baptismal rites of the more well-off were noisy too — but they were more subdued, with an occasional long wail of the infant or yelp of glee from an older sibling after the baptism. Sometimes we could hear the processions from the nearby village outside the abbey wall. But this morning was quiet and peaceful.

When the hawk was out of sight, I watched the orange and pink tint fade entirely – leaving white wisps of clouds stretched across morning blue sky. A flock of smaller birds flew into the sky in the form of a "V." I could hear the other birds in the treetops singing their morning sounds. At first, they just sounded like chirps. But as I listened further, I heard that the sounds of their calls were distinct. There was a long sound, then another long sound. I heard two short trills followed by a long one. I wondered what the birds were saying to each other. Maybe they were letting the others know that the hawk had passed and that the coast was clear. Maybe they were reciting poetic meter — in hexameters — to each other. I wondered if they were singing in Latin or Greek. It was probably Greek. I had started memorizing the Greek alphabet and the penultimate character (before *omega*) *psi* looked just like a bird's foot in reverse. If a bird was lying on its back with its feet straight up in the air, its feet would look like the *psi* character with a long thin line turning into three prongs at the top.

I wondered what my Latin teacher would say if he knew I was hearing hexameter in the birdsongs. I fantasized that he might be proud. Then I realized that he no doubt would think me pagan for feeling God in nature. I didn't want to be pagan, but I couldn't deny how I felt.

Maybe the pagans were just honoring God in their own way. I couldn't say that out loud though — especially to the Priest. He would certainly condemn me as a heretic.

Thinking of the Priest and his views on paganism reminded me of my beloved unicorn. I had intentionally not been looking for her. For one thing, I didn't want to invite heresy on myself. But I knew that it did not matter if I saw the unicorn again if I were by myself. I had to be with others — specifically the hunters who reported to the Bishop and the King — to get ahead. Now I had backed myself into a corner. I had to get ahead or be condemned as a heretic, or perhaps worse, just another fanciful poet. I told myself that I did not want to see the unicorn unless I was with someone to whom I could prove her existence. But deep in my gut, I knew I didn't want to see her, because I could not look her in the eye again without feeling guilty, guilty, guilty.

Just last week, I had talked to the Bishop. When the Priest told me that the Bishop wanted to meet with me, I had trembled with anticipation. But as it turned out, my expectations were dashed when I met the Bishop. I was afraid that I would be in such awe of him that I wouldn't be able to speak. After all, the Bishop was ordained by God. But he turned out to be quite an ordinary man. But I could tell he was a Bishop by the crimson robe — inset with vertical black panels — that he wore. And I could tell he was a busy man because he kept glancing at his wrist for some reason and mentioning that he had an *important* meeting soon. The way he said "important" made me feel dismissed. But maybe that was because I was just a simple monk and he was a high-ranking man of importance.

The Bishop told me that he wanted me to go out with the hunting party. I have never liked hunters. In fact, I couldn't think of a more unsavory way to pass the time. I found the thought of killing animals for sport to be barbaric. The idea of eating animals didn't appeal to me either. When I was a child, we almost never ate meat. Even though my father was a skilled craftsman, we were poor. As a monk, I don't have much occasion to each meat or fowl. But if the food usually reserved for priests and bishops were put in front of me, I can't say I wouldn't eat it. I might eat it out of politeness or from curiosity since there were so many delicacies I hadn't tried yet. I didn't want to be a hypocrite, so I decided to go with the hunters. But I hesitated when I opened my mouth to tell the Bishop that I would go with the hunters. I sensed that the Bishop suspected that I didn't want to go with the hunters. He was right. I wanted nothing less than to join the hunters.

However, I realized that my association with the unicorn — and the fact that I had bragged to the Priest about it — could work against me as well as in my favor. If I refused to cooperate in proving the unicorn was real, I would be thought of as a liar. If I told the Bishop that I did not care for hunters, he would think — and I was sure would tell the Priest — that I was weak. I would be a monk forever and no one would listen to me. If only I had never told the Priest that I had seen the unicorn.

I ignored the knot in my stomach and agreed to go with the hunters. I joined them when they were near the tall marble fountain in the middle of the abbey. I had been listening to the sound of water cascading against stone. It's a distinct, lulling and flowing sound. I wasn't surprised by the sight of men with javelins. The Bishop had told me that some hunters never went anywhere without their javelins. He told me that it was a matter of style. When I protested that they might hurt the unicorn, the Bishop had assured me that they would never hurt the unicorn. He said that the hunters would scare the creature into coming with them so that they could prove to the king that my theory was right, and the creature actually did exist. When he mentioned the King, the Bishop's eyes gleamed. He looked like a greedy man beholding a bag of gold. At first, I thought he looked this way because he was thinking about me — about the fact that I would be recognized — finally. The king would realize that I was important, someone to be listened to. But I've since thought this over. Why would an important Bishop be thinking about a lowly monk? His eyes most likely gleamed because he was thinking about himself. Perhaps he planned to use my proof that the unicorn existed to curry favor for himself with the King. After all, it was one of *his* monks that led him to the unicorn. But I told myself that I didn't mind the Bishop taking credit for my discovery as long as I benefitted as well. I had been around enough monks and priests to know that's how things worked: you scratch my back and I'll scratch yours. Maybe this was why I believed the Bishop when he told me that the javelins didn't matter and that the hunters wouldn't hurt the unicorn.

Perhaps I had overlooked too much.

When I was with the Bishop, I did the unthinkable. I wanted to impress him so much. His glittering ruby ring so mesmerized me that I didn't think about the vows of poverty. No doubt, his title impressed me too. He was the Bishop after all. For whatever reasons, I told him about the clearing. To him this was just a place. But to me it was a sacred place where I had seen the unicorn twice — once as a lad and once as a young monk.

I told him about the light shining down from the heavens. I told him about my fascination with the creature. I told him everything — almost everything. I did not tell him that seeing the unicorn made me aroused. If I told him that — or anyone — it could be taken out of context. I was aroused only in nature and the unicorn was the epitome of nature. Though to tell you the truth, I have often thought that I became aroused because I saw God when I looked at the unicorn. I had seen something that many have said doesn't exist. I had heard the angels bearing trumpets. Arousal was my body's way of telling me that what I saw was holy and good — that I was holy and good.

But I sensed the Bishop would never understand this or, like the Priest, he would say that such thinking was pagan and therefore heretical.

I told him *almost* everything. But I sensed he may have suspected the rest. The second time that I slipped and referred to my unicorn as "she" rather than the customary "he," I was afraid he had gone too far. But he didn't seem to be thinking about pronouns.

The Bishop narrowed his eyes at me and said, "My son, the unicorn is a *symbol* of Christ. He is not Christ himself."

I nodded gravely as if I agreed. I could not tell him that to me the unicorn was just as important as Christ — or more so. I could not tell him that I thought about the unicorn almost all the time and that when I looked heavenward, I saw the unicorn in the clouds.

While lost in my thoughts I had wandered way past my destination. I had been headed to the library, in the church. I had gone right past the church and was almost to the end of the abbey at the East wall. Perhaps I wandered there intentionally. This was one of my favorite places. The grounds were more overgrown. Vines wound around trees. The grass was higher. I could feel it tickling my toes in my sandals. I looked down and saw the periwinkle face of a wildflower smiling up at me.

Perhaps the quietness had to do with the fact that the nuns were nearby and that they had taken a vow of silence. I stood still for a moment and listened. I heard the rustle of wind in the tree branches and the grass. I heard the hum of the insects. I heard the chirp of a passing bird. I heard another bird responding. Perhaps they were warning each other about my presence. Then I heard something that I almost never hear in the abbey. It was the sound of female voices. Two women whispered. I could hear their voices distinctly. One had a deeper voice and the other one was higher. I didn't want to scare them, so I hid behind the medlar bush. The branches were in front of my eyes, so I couldn't see much but I could just make out the white habits of the two nuns. One was shorter than the other.

"I just don't think it's right," said the short one with the deeper voice. "The Mother Superior definitely knows something."

"But we're not alone. Remember Sister Beatrice?" The tall one with the higher voice spoke. I was careful to stay perfectly still. The longer I stood there, the more I could see and hear. I realized that the taller nun had the higher voice.

"The Sister who ran off with the carpenter?" answered the other one.

"Yes," said the other nun, the one with the higher voice. "She left suddenly, and we never saw her again."

"What does she have to do with us?"

"She must have fallen in love — like us," said the taller nun with the higher voice.

I was listening to blasphemy. I wanted to turn away. But I sensed that I couldn't without being detected. I stayed, still as a statue, and listened to what I shouldn't be hearing.

"But that's different," answered the shorter one with the deeper voice. "She fell in love with a man — a carpenter like Jesus."

"It's not different," the nun with the higher voice answered. "We all took vows. Love is love. And I love you. I joined the convent because nothing else was available to women — except marriage. My father wanted to marry me off when I was young, but then he listened to my pleas. I told him that I did not want to get married. I also told him that I wanted to join the convent to be closer to God. Both are true. I did not —and do not — want to marry a man. I am closer to God, because I found God in you. I imagine that our Sister feels the same way about her carpenter."

"I'm sure she does," the one with the deeper voice replied. "I feel the same way about you. God is love, and you are my love. But if we were man and women things would be different."

"That's true," the tall one with the higher voice replied. She sounded thoughtful. "If we were man and woman, we would be able to run away together… I have never heard of two women running off together, much less two nuns."

"Wait a minute –" The shorter nun with the deeper voice sounded excited and triumphant all at once. "What is stopping us from running away together to join the Poor Clares? I hear the order has really grown. We can find out which abbey to go to and make plans to leave together."

The taller one looked down at her lover sadly. "What difference will it make if we run to another order? I'm sure there is not one in the world where it does not matter if two nuns love each other. I have heard of priests who love other men. But it is forbidden for them also — even though they are men and things seem easier for them. Men can more easily go out into the world. They are builders and explorers. They can become priests and bishops and even popes. They have authority. Even if they cannot love each other, people listen to them."

"Yes, they do," replied the shorter one. "What can we do? We are only women and must stay in our place. And if we dare to step out of it, there will always be a mother superior to put us back in line."

"But we could still make it work between us," replied the taller one with the higher voice. "Maybe we can just stop sitting near each other at dinner and signing up for the same work shifts."

"But the Mother Superior would still know," argued the shorter one. "In fact, she may suspect that we are trying to trick her."

"The Mother Superior is not as all-seeing as you think she is," snapped the nun with the higher voice. "I know how to handle her."

There was silence.

Then I heard the nun with the higher voice sounding contrite.

"I'm sorry," she said. "I shouldn't have said that."

"No. You're right," replied the shorter one. "But there's more to it. This doesn't feel right. I love you more than I love Jesus."

She was still whispering, but her voice was harsher. She broke off in a sob.

I stood still as a statue but raised my eyebrows. What I heard — two nuns talking to each other, two nuns professing romantic love to each other — may have been blasphemy. Surely, these women were heretics. If discovered, they would be burned at the stake. But what the one said — about loving the other one more than she loved Jesus – resonated with me. This was how I felt about my beloved unicorn. Guilt consumed me.

Chapter Twelve

Dust motes floated in the shaft of light filtering down from the high window. The library was just a large room, filled with shelves and old books and some scrolls, in the outer hall of the church. To me, it represented worlds ancient and new.

After my eyes adjusted to the dimness, I reached for the book on a high shelf and examined its leather spine. In Latin it read "Saint Aquinas." Inspired by the hymns of Aquinas, I was eager to start reading his works. My teacher had mentioned that we would be studying Aquinas's theory of pre-destination. Truth be told, I had more interest in Aquinas's philosophy of goodness. Next to the Aquinas book were some other tomes with Latin titles. The names of the authors were on the leather spines: Cicero, Virgil, Tacitus.

Just then a book on the shelf beneath the Aquinas tome caught my eye. I lowered my reach and slowly retrieved it. It was about the same size as the Aquinas book. It was bound in leather also. It was much older than most of the books. The parchment binding was lighter in places where the exterior had – either through wear or simply the passing of time – started to crumble away. I noticed that there was no title on the spine. I blew the dust off the front cover. There were some round blank spaces. It looked like adorning gems were once on the cover and had been pried off long ago. The title was in Greek. I had just started to learn a few Greek words. Here was my chance to practice. I read the letters. There was a capital *Pi* followed by a *lambda* and an *alpha* with an accent above it, then a *tau*, and an *omega* followed by the lower case "v" character. The "v" character in Greek was pronounced "nu" as in none. I sounded the word out in my mouth several times — before I realized the direct translation: Plato. The ancients must have pronounced Plato's name as "Platon."

My stomach growled. I had just arrived at the library. Most of the morning had already gone by. I had been so excited that I was headed to the library, I hadn't eaten a thing. Taking a deep breath, I willed the hunger to go away. I walked over to the nearest desk. Since there was no chair, I hunched over the desk and gingerly opened the book to the beginning. I stared at the line in the middle of the otherwise blank opening page. The words looked familiar although they were written in a language that was new to me. Even so, I read the line carefully, remembering that in Classical Greek, the verb often comes at the end of the sentence. The sentence started with a capital "H" with an accent mark after it. I read each word carefully, sounding out the syllables and making the shapes with my mouth that combined with my breath would produce sounds. The Greek letter brought forth the sounds of the ancient alphabets that had preceded it — the pillars marked with Egyptian hieroglyphs and the native tongue of the Phoenician merchants. The Greek alphabet was reflected in the Latin that I had just learned. Most notable the Greek character *alpha* was replaced by the Latin letter *A*. But now it was clear that the letters that were different were related also. For instance, the third character of the Greek alphabet *gamma* had become the third alphabet character in Latin, *C*. When I sounded out the

Greek words, the language had a musical quality. It suddenly occurred to me that I recognized this phrase in the library book from the Greek primer that I had found in the library and read so much that I had some of it memorized.

"The soul is apparently immortal." – Plato

I thought about the fact that Plato, the *pagan* philosopher, had been the first — or one of the first — to write this down. Not only the sounds and forms of the language came springing forth in the Greek characters, but also the ideas. Plato was called a pagan philosopher because he had philosophized and written his thoughts a good three hundred years before the birth of Christ. I wondered if Plato worshipped the pagan gods, if he secretly worshipped the God of the Jews, or if he bowed down to none. I knew, of course, that Socrates was his teacher. The Priest had told me that Socrates said very little about the soul of a human being.

I had just started reading about Plato. My teacher knew more about Aristotle, but then he started reading and teaching Plato also. There were volumes written on Aristotle largely because Aquinas rescued him from oblivion. But it was known that Plato was Aristotle's teacher and therefore some scholars started researching and writing about Plato.

My teacher always emphasized that Plato came first because he was Aristotle's teacher. That was all he said. I distinctly got the impression that he was thinking of himself as a teacher – that HE should get the credit, not his student. Of course, Plato had a teacher — Socrates — but apparently there were no books written by Socrates or no writings that were saved. The Priest told me that he preferred Plato because of his statement, "The soul is eternal."

When we were talking, I had just been about to point out the obvious — that this view must have existed a long time before Christianity — when my teacher told me that it was obvious that Plato had a religious sensibility and if he had been born later, he would have been a Christian.

My teacher told me that Plato believed that aspiring to goodness (even if one couldn't always achieve it) was the most direct route to happiness. This was one of the moments when I looked at my teacher with awe. He was so wise. I had never thought about this before, but those who are happy are, by definition, not suffering.

The Priest added that Plato mentioned God along with gods and goddesses. When he said "goddesses" the Priest rolled his eyes. Then he said that Plato wrote of his own Grecian culture and of the Phoenician civilization in ancient Canaan, part of what became Israel, which proved that Plato knew his history. The Priest added that in addition to laying some of the ground work for Christianity, he would have been familiar with the beliefs of the Jews, many of whom were part of the Phoenician civilization.

The Priest stated that "the good" in Plato's philosophy — though he philosophized from a pagan perspective — no doubt laid down the foundation for the Christian philosophers led by Saint Augustine. He told me that Saint Augustine gave ample credit to Plato as well as Aristotle and Cicero in his opus *The City of God.* Then he added that the second part of the title, often dropped, is *Against the Pagans.* When I commented to the Priest that I found it odd that Saint Augustine cited the pagan philosophers in a book that he wrote to refute the pagans, the teacher looked bored and countered, "It makes perfect sense to me that he would have to know his enemies. The Bible tells us to love our enemies — this means that we have to be wise to what they have to teach us."

This was one of those moments when I had simply nodded. My teacher's statement was so profound that I had nothing to say.

Now, he added, as an afterthought, he warned me that when I talk to others, I should take care not to appear to have heretical thoughts.

I was quiet then because I felt I had said enough. I did not want the Priest to think me headed for heresy. But I was thinking that Plato must have gotten his idea about the immortal soul from somewhere — probably from paganism, Judaism, or both. Whoever passed down this knowledge must have gotten their wisdom from those who went before them. Perhaps their mothers had schooled them in matters of the eternal soul. Then Christianity came along and declared that the immortal soul had become life everlasting and that this started with Christianity. I knew that I could never tell anyone my thoughts — especially my teacher.

In the library, the thin parchment of the page looked fragile, so I carefully turned the page of the book on the table in front of me and re-examined the opening phrase in Greek that I recognized. Then I scrutinized the Greek words below it. I recognized *"Kallipolis"* — the hypothetical city state of which Plato wrote. I recognized the words — wisdom, courage, justice.

Then I recognized the Greek word for sun, *Helios*. It was spelled just like it sounded, with a capital *Eta* (resembling the Latin *H*), followed by a lower-case *epsilon*, and then the lower cases of *lambda, iota, omega* and *sigma*. I looked at the word again and was reminded of my story of my sighting of the unicorn. The brightness of *Helios*, the sun, reminded me of the light that emanated from the unicorn. My mother had taught me that *Helios* was a God and was once worshipped as a personification of the sun. The great poets, Homer included, wrote that each day *Helios* drove a chariot of sun around the earth.

The Greek letters in the book were handwritten. They must have been copied from scroll to scroll and then finally to a book. Perhaps a monk like me had done the calligraphy after he had learned Greek.

My thoughts strayed from my epic to my beloved unicorn. The Greeks had long believed that the unicorn was real. I knew she was real, but it was nice to have my belief confirmed. To tell you the truth, she was always in my thoughts. It might be mostly imaginary, but she was my friend, my companion — not only a gentle presence but someone who let in the light. I hoped she wouldn't be too angry when she was captured alive and brought to the king in proof that she existed. Somehow, I would tell her that this was for the good of everyone: the knowledge of her existence would travel and bring peace ever after to all the lands. How could it not?

I closed the book but found myself opening it again to the front page which had the quote on it. I mentally translated the Greek: "*The soul is apparently immortal. —Plato*"

I wondered what he meant by using the word "apparently." A great philosopher, he would have chosen his words carefully. Perhaps he meant that this seemed to be the case, but that skepticism was part of thinking and that the ability for critical thinking was what made us human.

I examined the Greek letters again. I couldn't wait to learn more. I imagined the worlds — and the secrets — that learning the language would unlock.

Just then I heard a sound. I listened and heard it again. Was it mice? I hoped they didn't bring a new outburst of the plague.

I closed the book soundlessly and listened.

I heard it again. It sounded like snuffling — not scuttling. I was relieved that the sound was human rather than vermin. Still, how did I not know that someone else was in the library? Could I have been that lost in my thoughts?

I tiptoed toward the sound, peered around several bookshelves and saw a monk bent over in the back of the room. His back trembled and his shoulders shook. It looked like he was crying.

I couldn't tell who it was. All I saw at first was a brown-hooded robe. But then he turned toward me, just slightly. I saw sandy hair sticking like straw out of the top of the hood and then the profile of a square jaw.

Gregory? Could it be? I was beside myself with curiosity.

He was clutching the front of his robe and bringing it up to dry his eyes.

The snuffling got louder. Clearly the young man was breaking down in sobs.

What could it be that had upset him so?

I wondered briefly if he was crying over Thomas.

My love was different — I didn't feel like I had given my heart away — but my devotion to my beloved unicorn gave me insight.

I knew enough about human nature to know that if Gregory had broken the heart of our teacher by choosing Thomas, then it wouldn't be surprising if Thomas had broken Gregory's heart.

But my main thought concerned Gregory's mind — not his heart. The beautiful young man who seemed to rely on his looks for a good grade in Latin class — was in the *library*.

I felt like running up to him, hugging him and telling him that everything would be okay. I even thought of telling him that Thomas had done him a favor. Look where he was: the library!

Then I would point him in the direction — of where? Perhaps, I would direct him to the most basic Latin primer.

But I knew that wouldn't be appropriate. My instincts told me he would hate me for seeing him like this. It was a good thing that I had been quiet. He didn't know that Father Matthew had confided in me about him. He may ask me how I knew so much about his life, and I might end up breaking a confidence.

But something good did come from me finding Gregory in this state. I had wondered what my calling would be. But I hadn't given it much thought lately — with concentrating on my studies and scheming how to get ahead through proving the existence of the unicorn.

But now I knew what my calling was. I was destined to become a teacher. I would encourage my students to read. I would teach them that by reading, they would hold the world in their hands.

Chapter Thirteen

"I thought that today we could discuss the theory of Natural Law that Thomism espouses," I settled into my chair across from my teacher's desk.

Father Matthew's eyebrows shot up. He dropped his quill pen.

"It sounds like someone's been doing some reading — *before* I assigned the material about St. Aquinas." He frowned as he answered.

"Yes, just last week, I went to the library and found a book on St. Aquinas. It was quite fascinating," I answered and then added: "I began to be intrigued by Saint Thomas Aquinas when I heard his beautiful hymns at vespers."

The Priest nodded, and then looked at me shrewdly.

I couldn't help blurting out what I thought was good news: that I had done some studying on my own. But I didn't tell him that I went to the library whenever I could – at least a few times a week — and that I had started to learn Greek. I didn't tell him that my initial motivation for wanting to learn Greek — though the language itself now fascinated me – was because I wanted to be a priest like him so that I could be a teacher and so that people would listen to me. I didn't tell him any of this, because I sensed that my ambition might threaten him.

He shifted in his chair, narrowed his eyes and spoke: "*I planned for our discussion today to more directly relate to our current studies. There's no point in jumping ahead.*"

I nodded.

Father Matthew smiled at me, pleased at my acceptance of his authority. What choice did I have?

"I know you are eager to learn, and I know you have goodness in your heart. Saint Aquinas would approve. But before we learn about goodness, we have to learn about sin."

I raised my eyebrows. *Really?* I thought. I said nothing.

"As the great Christian philosopher Saint Augustine wrote, we first have to understand sin to understand goodness," he continued.

"Why is that sir?" I was feeling peeved that he hadn't taken my direction to talk about St. Thomas Aquinas, but this was taken over by my feelings of remorse. Who was *I* to try to direct my discussion with the Priest who knew so much more than I?

"The first thing to remember is that we are all sinners," said the Priest, sagely.

"What do you mean?" I asked, innocently. I really did want to know.

I had heard this, too, from my other Priest, from when I was a lad growing up in the village, but what did this really mean? If we were all sinners, then why did we hear so much about sin? Wasn't it a moot point?

"The church's position is called 'Original Sin.' It is based on the fact that we are all sinners because we descended from Adam," explained the Priest. "We are all sinners because he was a sinner starting when he ate the forbidden fruit and was cast out of the Garden of Eden."

I nodded. This made sense. But then I thought of something: "But didn't God make Adam from a pile of dust. Does this mean that God's a sinner too?"

"Of course not," answered the Priest. He looked at me sternly as if I were being preposterous. "God created Adam as an innocent. Adam was without sin but then he went and ate from the tree of knowledge — *on Eve's advice.*

"I see, Adam is a sinner because he listened to Eve," I replied. The Priest smiled and nodded. "Now you're getting it. Women are a corrupting influence on men. It's in the Bible."

Sometimes I just said what I knew the Priest wanted to hear. *Notice that I didn't say I agreed with him.* But I knew it was futile to argue the point. He'd probably just say that I missed my mother — (in the process imply that I was acting like a baby) — and that's why I took the side of women. He'd probably ridicule me by saying what he said before, that I was getting too old for that.

But I *did* miss my mother. I didn't think I'd ever get too old for that. She was the pure goodness that I sought in wanting to study Saint Aquinas. For some reason, thinking about my mother made me think of my beloved unicorn. Like my unicorn, my mother was goodness — and radiated with pure light. Suddenly, I felt the color rise in my cheeks. *Guilt.* I felt very guilty. How could I betray such a creature? I had my own interests foremost in my mind. I was no better than the others who schemed to get ahead – whether it was the good-looking monks trying to catch the teacher's eye or the older priests and bishops wheeling and dealing to curry favor.

The Priest looked at me with compassion — as if he knew my thoughts.

"You are young and have lived a sheltered life. But even if you are unacquainted with sin personally, you are still a descendant of Adam. You are still a sinner."

When the Priest said that I was a sinner, I felt *very* bad. Not only did I betray my beloved unicorn. But I lied to the

Bishop when I omitted the fact that I was aroused by the unicorn. Wasn't omission the same thing as lying? I knew that lying was a sin. That meant that I was a sinner. And I had lied to the Bishop no less. He was still a church father — regardless what I thought about his finery and his glittering rings not to mention what I imagined about the scheming that he must have had to do to become a bishop.

"I just saw the Bishop less than a week ago," I said.

"Oh?" replied the Priest.

He had been acting bored, but now he was alert. I had his undivided attention. It seemed that mentioning the Bishop pre-empted sin in the Priest's mind. I'd have to remember that.

"You set up the meeting, remember?"

"That's right. He wanted to talk to you about the hunt for the mythical beast that you keep insisting is real," replied the Priest.

"She IS real," I responded. "I saw her again. The Bishop wanted me to go out with the hunting party to help them, so I did. I saw her near the fountain, and I pointed the men in her direction so that they could track her."

"Hmmm." The Priest seemed bored again. His eyes were starting to glaze over. "That reminds me… we'll have to cut our time together short today. I have another meeting."

I bristled. How could my mention of the unicorn remind him that he had another meeting?

"If only there was a way that you could tell time indoors," I said. I wanted to make him feel as frustrated as I was feeling.

"There is a way," said the Priest. "I saw it on the Bishop's wrist. He has a sundial on his wrist band and all he has to do is look at it to tell the time."

So that's why the Bishop kept looking at his wrist when I was with him. I hadn't known what it was. Who would!? Whoever heard of a sundial small enough to fit on your wrist?

"But," I said, pointing out the obvious, "if you had a sundial in this room, on your wrist or not, it wouldn't work because it is too dim."

"Then I would go outside and look at it," replied the Priest, crossly.

He did not like me raining on his parade.

"But then you would spend more time finding out the time. That means that you would have less time," I replied. "What is the point?"

"The point is that the Bishop has one and I want one too." The Priest sounded petulant, like a small child.

"But isn't desire sinful?" I asked, as innocently as I could.

"Yes, it is," declared the Priest. "And this proves the point that all of us are sinners. Not only did I illustrate desire, but I showed you what covetous means. The Bishop has a sundial on his wrist, and I want one. To covet is forbidden."

I had to work hard not to make a face of puzzlement. I could have sworn that the Priest really did want a sundial on his wrist because the Bishop had one. I didn't think he had been trying to make a point about sin.

"I see from your silence that I haven't convinced you that we are all sinners. Maybe it will help if I quote the Bible: 'He that is without sin among you, let him first cast a stone.' That is from the Gospel of John."

I could tell from the way that the Priest smiled at me triumphantly that he thought that by quoting the Bible, he would end the conversation. I was still smarting from the fact that he was going to cut our time short to go to another meeting. *I'll show him,* I thought.

"But stones are cast all the time," I countered. "And sometimes garbage is thrown also. Just before I left my parents' house in the forest, I walked by the town square and saw a man on the block with his head and hands in a pillory. A hooded man behind him was spanking him with a paddle."

"Really?"

"Yes," I replied. "He was being spanked by the guards for committing a petty offense. His face turned red from humiliation. It really was a sin."

Chapter Fourteen

I had left the stream where my friends, the lion, the meerkat, the hyena and the stag were drinking the water that I purified for them. But first I told the other animals about the hunting party that I saw that morning. I had no idea the hunters were so close, or I would have told the other animals to disband immediately. I had no idea the hunters were coming after me, but I knew that they were coming after someone — probably the majestic stag or the wily fox. I told the others to scatter in different directions after they had drunk their fill from the purified stream.

Just in case the hunters were coming after me, I planned on circling back, going to the place in the West where the abbey wall was low, scaling it, and heading toward the castle. I didn't know what was on the other side of the wall. There might have been other hunting parties for all I knew. If my memory was correct, I would have to skirt several villages where noisy, filthy people lived in hovels. Outside the towns were cemeteries filled with people who were even more noisy and filthy and who lived in tents. After I passed through the towns and cemeteries, I would come to the grove where I might find the warrior princess and her friends jousting.

Just then I heard a flock of birds in the sky calling to me. I could tell from the high sharp tones of their calls that I was in danger. *Danger, danger,* they called to each other. Then they flew away.

I looked after them wistfully. How I longed to be a drunken sparrow zigzagging in the sky — or any kind of bird drunk or not — even if I had to fly in formation. I knew with a kind of doom that I could not fly away. The sky had been clear earlier when I was at the fountain. But it was gray now. Dark clouds were rolling in. I sniffed the air. I did not detect the porous scent that comes before the rain though. It felt more ominous than a storm. Maybe the hunters had become so large in formation that they kicked up dust clouds.

The silence was ominous. I listened for the calls of new birds, for the rustling of a breeze, but I heard nothing.

But then I heard the crackle of hunters stomping through the underbrush behind me. My ears picked up their secret calls to each other: their trills, the deep windy sound the scout's horn made. I heard the yips of the hounds. They were probably being chased by hunters, some of whom were no doubt whipping them to make them run faster. I realized now, from my gut instincts, that I was the one being hunted – not my horned stag friend, not the absent red fox with his bushy tail and beady eyes. The hunters were coming for me. I could feel it in my bones.

I stopped by a stand of birch trees with some tall bushes — a medlar and two holly bushes — behind it. I pushed aside the shiny leaves of the holly and put my head down, so my horn would point toward the earth — instead of the sky — so that I would be better hidden.

I squinted until my eyes were shut. I pretended that I was invisible. Maybe if I could not see anything — the hunters would not see me.

I tried to think of something that would make me feel safe. My old friend the Great Lion popped into my mind. He was a close friend. I respected him very much. I was with him when he was dying. He was very old and hadn't been himself for some time. I sat nearby but not too close. Lions like their space. My friend was no exception. When he was dying, I just sat there quietly — watching him.

When I was sitting with him, I saw something out of the corner of my eye. I could have blinked and missed it. It was a vibration, a quiver of air that lifted from the Great Lion and kept rising in the sky — where it formed a rectangle — until it was no longer visible. I remember feeling strongly that the best part of him was going to a place where everything was perfect. There wouldn't be any hunters. The only king would be him. I distinctly remember being flooded with a sense of relief. My friend's ordeal was over. He could be himself now and do anything that he wanted. He could leap as high as he wanted. He could befriend humans as well as animals. Everyone would respect him. He would never go hungry.

I remember thinking that I would miss my friend, but I knew that I would find him in a mountain stream or beaming down in a shaft of light. His wisdom would always be with me.

Perhaps that's why I have never been afraid of death. I had never thought that death was something that might apply to me. Perhaps the two — thinking that you will die and fearing death — go together. I know that my wisdom is eternal and will resurface later in a cloud, a sunset or in another being. I might even be resurrected in a tapestry.

But I did fear these hunters. There was something greedy and futile in their blank stares that I had seen just this morning. They looked like they would keep hunting until all of us were gone — not only my kind who were scarce already but all the animals. They would never be happy until we were all hunted down or at least so afraid of them that we wanted to strike terror in their hearts also. And when they were done killing or imprisoning us, the men would turn on each other.

My eyes were still shut. The image of my old friend the Great Lion faded from my mind. It was replaced with an image of my young human friend. My eyes flew open. How could I have ever trusted a human? It came to me in a flash. He had desired me so badly that he wished me dead — either consciously or unconsciously. I had seen the greenish glow around him. Even then, I had been around long enough to know how things worked. What did he tell the hunters? Did he tell them that I existed? Did he tell them about my place in the clearing where he found me? Did he tell them that he spied me looking at my reflection? Did he tell them that he had glowed green with obsession?

I doubt that he told them everything.

The men probably had their own reasons for wanting to hunt me. But what were they? It was said that they wanted my horn. They thought that it was an antidote to poison and that it would cure all ailments. The wise old unicorn had told me that it was said that a piece of my horn in the mouth of a human corpse would bring the human back to life. But I knew they wanted something else. What did they want really? Did they want fame? Did they want glory? Did they want to please someone? Maybe it was their father. Maybe their mother told them old tales of seeing my kind deep in the woods. Maybe they wanted to please her. Maybe they wanted to refute her.

Why did they really want to hunt me?

What were they looking for?

Did they really want to kill me — or were they looking for something in themselves and trying to kill it?

Or were they just following orders and trying to impress each other?

I should have been moving on with urgency. I turned around but then turned back again. I was rethinking my plan of circling around to move outside the abbey walls and going toward the castle. I didn't want to lead the hunters to the warrior princess. Though, I'm sure that the princess and her handmaidens would take care of the hunters. The young women would have some live ones to practice on and I'm sure the men would end up wishing they never laid eyes on them.

I put my horn up, making sure that it was right next to the birch tree so that I would blend in with the white bark. Then I opened my mouth and muttered a spell that was a mystery to me, making it all the more powerful, and something that might save me:

> "*For I am knowledge and ignorance.*
> *I am shame and boldness.*
> *I am shameless; I am ashamed.*
> *I am strength and I am fear.*
> *I am war and peace.*
> *Give heed to me.*
>
> "*I am the one who is disgraced and the great one.*
> *Give heed to my poverty and my wealth.*
> *Do not be arrogant to me when I am cast out upon the earth,*
> *and you will find me in those that are to come.*
> *And do not look upon me on the dung-heap*
>   *nor go and leave me cast out,*
>   *and you will find me in the kingdoms.*
> *And do not look upon me when I am cast out among those who*
>   *are disgraced and in the least places,*
>   *nor laugh at me.*
> *And do not cast me out among those who are slain in violence.*

. . . .

"' am the knowledge of my inquiry,
*   and the finding of those who seek after me,*
*   and the command of those who ask of me,*
*   and the power of the powers in my knowledge*
*   of the angels, who have been sent at my word,*
*   and of gods in their seasons by my counsel,*
*   and of spirits of every man who exists with me,*
*   and of women who dwell within me.*
I am the one who is honored, and who is praised,
*   and who is despised scornfully."'*

Chapter Fifteen

En route to jumping over the abbey wall, I was suddenly surrounded by hunters. Intent on my destination, I was minding
my own business. I had just leapt across a tributary of the same
stream I had purified earlier. I've had a chance to study this
tapestry for eons. Still, I always see something new. Hunters
surrounded me on all sides. Looking at the tapestry again, I
see a hunter grasping a sturdy branch hanging above me. At
first, I think he is suspended from the tree but then I see that
he has grasped the branch and is emerging from the forest. The
branch is near the top of the tapestry, just under the oak leaves.
With his free hand he reaches toward a man in a red hat and
silver blue tunic bent forward slightly at the waist. This man
is holding a javelin with a metal tip that he is about to thrust
into my throat. At the top of the tapestry, a horizontal strip of
blue sky leads to the castle in the upper-right hand corner. I
was headed toward the castle — to the grove where I thought
I'd find the warrior princess and her handmaidens. I still had
hope then that they would save me. The branch near the top of
the tapestry extends from a mighty oak planted in the ground
beneath the stream at the bottom of the tapestry. I am charging
through the stream with my back legs in the water. My forelegs
above the banks of the stream are poised to gallop onto solid

ground. There were dogs to each side of me in the stream. Even though I've stared at this tapestry hanging on the wall across from me for so long, I really haven't studied some pieces of the scene before me. I look delirious with my tongue sticking out of my mouth slightly. I must have been panting and out of breath. My memory is hazy, but it must have been extremely frightening, not to mention psychically painful, to have been suddenly ambushed like that. It appears that I would never be able to escape the hunters and their javelins and their dogs and scale the West wall like I had intended — to find the warrior princess who I still thought would save me.

Despite that I rarely, if ever, hurt others, I knew I would have to defend myself soon. What choice did I have?

I'm looking for my human "friend" in this tapestry. He pointed me out in the last tapestry when I was near the fountain. But he isn't in this tapestry. I don't know that this is to his benefit. It's true that since he isn't in this new picture of me — surrounded by hunters and their dogs as I leap over the stream — that maybe he had no knowledge that the hunters were going to try to kill me. I remember giving the hunters the benefit of the doubt. Maybe they were just going to capture me and take me to the warrior princess to be her pet. Surely, she would free me. One of the hounds had bit my back. I remember feeling a warm trickle of blood traveling down my hind quarters. I had smelled the metallic scent of blood — this meant the hounds must have smelled it as well.

It really doesn't matter that my young "friend" isn't there. His absence speaks volumes. If he was truly honorable, he would have come to save me. "Stop," he could have said. On that one command, the history of the world could have been changed. Maybe. The hunters might have ignored him. What use was he to them now? They might have been so full of blood lust and the desire to impress each other that they might have just gone ahead with their javelins and their hounds in pursuit of me. Who knows?

Maybe when I saw him pointing at me in the last tapestry — when I was innocently kneeling under the fountain and purifying the stream with my horn — he was merely doing what he was asked to. Undoubtedly, he had his reasons for pointing me out. Maybe he thought that this was his only path to fame and glory. But even so, wouldn't this make him a coward? A valiant friend would have pointed the hunters in the other direction. But maybe he was afraid that if they did not find me, the hunters would come for him.

To give him the benefit of the doubt — maybe he thought the hunters were just going to capture me and take me to the King to be a pet for the warrior princess. Maybe he, too, thought that she was certain to set me free.

Regardless, it is hard for me to admit that it's partly my fault. If I hadn't shown myself to the young human and encouraged him to desire me — I wouldn't be in this predicament of jumping the stream with hunters all around me. Or would I?

Is it my fault I existed?

What about the hunters — is there anything I could have done to have made them go away?

At the bottom of the tapestry is a stretch of green. Now that I have time to look, I recognize the medlar bush with its small, dusty-orange fruits, several oak tree seedlings and some of my favorite baby herbs to munch on — including the dusty sage and the tall, feathery deep purple flowers of the clary.

I see two birds now — one looking at the hunters calmly and the other pecking at the ground. Both are small and an identical light tan in color. One is sitting upright and gazing calmly in the direction of the hunters behind me. The other one is in the very front of the scene, at the bottom of the tapestry, bending over and pecking at the earth. It looks like this bird is on the scent of a worm.

Past the base of the mighty oak that springs from the bottom of the tapestry, to the right of the birds, are two ducks. They are in various stages of landing in the stream below me and floating on it as ducks do. These ducks are not mallards. There are no distinctive rings about their necks. These are rather plain ducks — one is dark brown, the other a lighter tan. It is a rather nice part of the scene — these undisturbed birds and ducks, going about their lives as if there is not a major disruption nearby. But there is something off about this.

The birds and the ducks would never have been this close to the hunters and their dogs. If they just happened to be there when the hunters and their dogs suddenly appeared, the birds and the ducks would have flown away to safety. But the ducks are shown landing on the stream — not flying away from it.

The tapestry maker must have been torn between wanting to show the beauty of the land — the setting — and the awful realistic violence of the hunt with me in the center. I do have to admit that I make it all more interesting.

Aside from the tall oak tree which runs through the center of the tapestry, I am directly in the center. I am the focal point. The hunters are all around me and they are focused on me. They look as if they know they are lucky to have found me.

Even though I was surrounded, I was willing to give them the benefit of the doubt. If they had just disappeared — if they had gone back to the hovels with their wives or crept away into the forest with each other, I would have given them no more thought. I would have wished them well. I would have bowed in their direction and sent them happiness. If they were truly happy, they would not be trying to hunt me down.

If they were truly happy, they would unleash their dogs and set them free.

Happiness could rule the world. But it seems there is always a tyrant — who is denying his own happiness as well as everyone else's — vying to rule over all the lands.

I'd like to think that I could have shown the hunters how to be happy. But that was not what happened. Each person's happiness is up to that individual. Happiness comes from the voice that can only be heard from within. Unfortunately, it is far easier for people to listen to the loudest voices among them. And this voice never brings happiness.

But as I gaze at this tapestry now, looking intently at the image of myself leaping over the stream, I am forced to acknowledge the force of goodness that I bring to the world. I am beautiful. I am unusual. I am not armed. I am the center of the tapestry.

I am at the center of all that is good.

Chapter Sixteen

Somehow, I got free. My memory is so murky that I would be telling an untruth — at the very least a fabrication — if I told you I knew how I did it. Judging from the tapestry — and the nearness of the castle in the upper right-hand corner — I must have seen an opening and ran for it. I burst forth from the ambush of hunters, with their spear tipped javelins and blood-thirsty hounds, and galloped toward the West wall, which is lower than the rest of the wall, toward the distant castle.

Then I jumped over the wall as if I were a tournament horse performing a trick or maybe more like a flying horse — like Pegasus. Sometimes fear gives you wings. I was still bleeding. I could feel the trail of warm liquid on my back. No doubt the hounds were on the scent of my blood. But I was free.

I knew just the clearing where I would find the warrior princess jousting with her handmaidens. I felt secure in the knowledge that the warrior princess would set me free. But first I had to get through the forest.

After I entered the thick cover of trees, I slowed. You might say that I ambled. The hunters might be on my scent, but they would never find me here. This was my territory. The only humans who had ever found me here were the wild women — the ones who had been my friends since they were virginal maidens. Many rode me in the past. Today I felt a human presence behind a leafy bush. I did not feel threatened, so I slowed and sniffed. The scent was unmistakably female – but she was not a maiden. I crinkled my nose and stopped.

A woman with long brown locks woven into two braids and smiling eyes stepped from behind the bush. A pale pink flower adorned one of her braids, just above her right ear.

"I remember you," she said sweetly. "I rode you when I was a maiden and then again later when I was older."

In a flash she took off her clothes. Naked, she leapt onto my back. Even though we had done this before, I was startled by the fact that she was on my back – maybe I was still spooked by the hunters – and I ran very fast. Before I knew it, I had bolted through the woods. I was startled, but I remembered this woman by the weight of her on my back. She was heavy – but not too heavy. Her breathing was ragged, even though I was the one doing the running. I could feel her jerk her head away from the low hanging tree branches.

I stopped abruptly. I was simply done having a rider – with no reason. I feared that she would tumble forward. But she was as gentle as the wind. She disembarked quickly and as she did, she whispered to me. I had no idea what she was saying but her soft voice was soothing — as I trotted away. Then she was gone. I was as amazed as she was. I knew that women like her existed. But they were as rare as me. Whenever a wild woman rode me, it just kind of happened. This woman disappeared suddenly when she dismounted me. I wondered briefly if she had really been there. I thought that maybe I had imagined her, but the place where her thighs pressed my back was still warm. And the pressed pink flower that she had worn in her hair was at my feet. A low hanging vine must have swept it loose.

I was so immersed in my reverie of meeting the wild woman that I almost walked into a low-hanging branch. I skirted the branch deftly and continued. I departed from the path and entered the dark thickness of the forest. There was barely any light in the forest — even though it was a sunny day. The forest was that overgrown. I did not need my sight to guide me. I went by touch. The ground under me felt soft and mossy. My horn — held high — lightly touched branches. I twisted and turned as I moved through the forest. A vine caught my horn. I sliced through it. I went on like that for a while. Then I saw light filtering through the branches of trees. I slowed and approached the light — brighter now and shooting from behind the trees in several directions. The rays of the light reminded me of a majestic star hanging in the pristine night sky. I saw such a star once, in the silent snowy winter, but that is another story. I thought I had reached the other edge of the forest, but as I entered the light, I could see a clearing that formed the perfect symmetry of a square.

I stopped and listened, sniffed and heard a human voice.

A small but sturdy-looking house sat directly in the middle of the clearing.

I heard someone singing. The voice was high and melodious — much like the voices that come out of the church inside the abbey. But I could tell this voice was from a woman — not the high tones of a man. When I heard a solo voice singing in the abbey church, I could tell it was a man singing — even if the tone was high — because the melody had a thick throaty sound.

The peals that I heard were those of a woman who is not only satisfied with her life, but grateful for each moment — not only for the fresh air that she breathed — but for everything that had brought her to this breath. I was entranced. I don't usually get that close to humans — unless I am lying my head in a maiden's lap. But there was something familiar about this voice. Maybe I had lain my head in this maiden's lap. I felt compelled to find out. I approached the little house. I knew I could easily turn and run back into the forest where it was dark, where humans could not see and where I was protected by the sense of touch that guided me. I looked in the window and did a double take. At first, I thought I must be seeing a reflection — for I was looking at myself or a creature who looked remarkably like me. I have to say, I was quite taken with the beauty of this creature. It must have been me.

Then I noticed that it wasn't a reflection. It was a weaving that was still on the loom. A woman was sitting before it. Her back toward me, I could see her shining hair and hear the other-worldly tones of her voice as she sang her mesmerizing song. I could feel my lips twitching and the ends turning up. I rarely smile — even though I find almost everything slightly amusing.

But what I saw was so funny that it made me smile. The weaving in front of the woman depicted me — or someone who strongly resembled me — in a wooden pen. There was a thick collar around the neck of the creature who looked like me. The pattern of the collar looked like the circles on a peacock's tail feathers and it matched the golds, greens, and pinks of the foliage and flowers. It looked like someone had chained the creature to a tree behind it. I could see the thin links of a thin golden chain.

It was ludicrous to think that such a chain could hold me — or any creature like me for that matter. One yank of my muscular neck would take care of that flimsy chain. It was also ludicrous to even think — nonetheless weave the image — of me allowing someone to place a collar around my neck.

I wasn't some domesticated animal — like a hound doing his master's bidding, and then turning around and begging with doleful eyes for a scrap or pat. The pen itself — although the wooden fence in a circle looked innocent enough — was so low that I could easily jump it. There I was sitting contentedly in the middle — my front and back legs stretched out, complacency on my face.

I realized that my twitching lips weren't curling into a smile – but a sneer.

The scene was ludicrous. Aside from that, it wasn't so much of a nice scene —although it looked rather serene — as a terrifying scene. I couldn't imagine ever allowing myself to be captured like that. I was a unicorn — proud and free. I was wild and elusive. I was unique. I was NOT someone's captured pet.

The woman stood, still with her back toward me. I could see now that was wearing a simple dress of burlap with a belted waist. A skirt fell past her ankles. I imagined that she was admiring her work. She was almost done and had woven nearly to the top of the pomegranate tree — the same one that held my image captive — that the slender golden chain was tied to.

Then the woman turned and in that fleeting moment — before I turned and ran back to the forest — I recognized her. She had the same luminous oval face that resembled the moon. Her face still radiated innocence. Before she had a worn a habit that covered her hair. But now her hair hung freely over her shoulders. It was the color of golden flax in the summer. She came toward the window and blinked with disbelief. She must have thought she was seeing things. Then she shrugged as if she had been sitting at her loom for too long and imagined that she had my image burned into her eyes.

By this time, I had scampered back to the forest, but could not bring myself to go far. I hid behind a tree and peered around it. I saw that she had come out of the front door and stood there singing as sweetly as a song bird. I recognized her as the young nun who had left the abbey to be with her carpenter. She must be waiting to him to return to her after his day's work.

She was the young maiden whose lap I had lain my head it – long ago it seemed. As I suspected, she no longer smelled like a virgin. I crinkled my nose. If she were still a virgin, I would smell that intoxicatingly sweet scent even from behind the tree. As it was, the breeze wafted a familiar but slightly acrid scent under my nose.

I crinkled my nose.

Then her carpenter came trudging into the clearing from the other direction.

She turned and waved. The glow around her brightened.

The light surrounded him too. They both had had long days. They looked tired. But the glow that pulsed around them as their lips met briefly, meant that they still were circled in love.

"It seems like you have been gone a long time," she said to him.

"I worry about you, Beatrice, here all day in the midst of the forest with wild animals all around," the man said with a concerned furrow in his brow.

Beatrice said nothing for a moment. Then she spoke:

"I worry about you too my love. Every day, when you walk through the woods to find work, you run the risk of being ambushed by bandits."

"Do not worry, love," he replied. "As a carpenter, I know the woods well — for I fell trees there. Besides, there are not as many bandits as there used to be." He paused and looked meaningfully at Beatrice. "We should just be thankful that we are not serfs."

"You are right, my lord. I am thankful, but I am still afraid," Beatrice answered.

"Maybe we should move to the village closer to the castle," replied the man. "We would probably have to move into a house that is already built — chances are that the houses are crooked — and would have to leave our sturdy home that I built for us. But at least you would be around people all day and you would be safer."

"But when I go to the village, people turn away from me as if I am a pariah. Word must have travelled. I will be forever known as that evil woman who scorned God. I am no better than a heretic — or a witch."

"But they do not know us," said the man. "In time—"

"They are afraid that God might disapprove and take out his wrath on them. Things have been good in the land. There hasn't been a crop failure in years. But there could be a famine right around the next corner. Chances are that it was going to happen anyway — without having anything to do with us. But you know how people are. They are afraid that their luck will change. They are only being human. They do not know what God has in store for them and they are afraid of displeasing Him. If there is too much rain or not enough or if an invasion of a foreign army destroys the crops, the townspeople will be looking around for someone to blame. They could blame us now for what might happen later."

"But maybe if we moved to the village and went to the church, things would be different. That way, they would get to know us and see that we are decent people." His voice trailed off as he spoke.

It sounded like he was pleading — as if this were not the first time, he had suggested this.

"I am not fit to enter a church," said Beatrice sadly. "I do not think that belonging to a church will help. The townspeople love to have someone to shun. It makes them feel better about themselves. Besides, I don't have to enter a church for God to hear my prayers. The order in the abbey taught me well. There I was able to walk in nature and feel the presence of God. As a result, I can pray in solitude. Not that my prayers are working. We have yet to bring a child into the world. When the midwife's charms didn't work, she said that God must be punishing me for leaving the order."

"She is just making excuses for the fact that her remedies don't help," said the carpenter. A red flush crept from his neck to his face. He trembled as he spoke. "Maybe it's time for you to find another midwife. This one is obviously incompetent."

The woman was silent, but she nodded and looked as though she hadn't thought of this before.

"You are right, my husband."

"Of course, I am," he replied. "Nothing is your fault. Besides, we don't know what God's plan is. Perhaps it is better that you remain childless right now because the risks of pregnancy are too great."

His wife bowed her head. "You are right again, my beloved. We have each other — there is no greater gift. I thank God every day that I found you. I believed in God before, but now you are my living proof that God exists."

"WE found each other," said the man tenderly but firmly. "I am thankful to God also. Although I don't pray as often as you. But I do see the reflection of God in you. My love for you is so great that it is nothing short of a miracle."

Behind my tree, I started. I must have been falling asleep standing up. I was glad things had worked out with the happy couple and hoped the villagers would come around. But I was thinking ahead to seeing the warrior princess and wanted to reach her grove before night fall. I hadn't seen her in a long time and was excited. Surely, she would be surprised and happy to see me!

The carpenter and his wife finally went in their little house. I heard some words about dinner — a leftover hunk of pig in the cold storage.

I shuddered. There was nothing worse than being a domesticated animal – except for being dinner.

I took the long way through the forest — to avoid the village — in the direction of the castle and the nearby secret grove where I might find the warrior princess.

When I arrived at the grove, I peered in and recoiled. Instead of the warrior princess jousting with her handmaidens, there a partially constructed round fence — just like the one the young wife had been weaving an image of in her little house.

A pomegranate tree was in the middle of the circle, too — just like in the weaving. There was even a collar and a fine gold chain lying on the ground. The only thing missing was me.

I felt the hairs on my mane bristle. Then I wondered if I looked good with bristling hair — for, as I am the first to admit, I am vain even in times of strife. Then I returned to feeling the horror of my feelings. Maybe the young wife in the clearing was prescient. Maybe she was a witch and could see the future. It was okay with me if she was a witch, but if what she saw in the future was correct, then it was terrifying. For I could never be anyone's pet. I could not even "belong" to the warrior princess. Maybe the King wanted me captured as a gift for his daughter. Perhaps she would release me. We both had to be free. My wish for the warrior princess was that she would grow up to be as free as the wild women in the woods. For if the King succeeded in taming her and turning her into some other king's queen, then what was the point?

If we aren't free to be ourselves, then why go on? The ones who are the same are interchangeable. But to be yourself — that is exhilarating!

I found the prospect of a fenced-in future impossible to bear, so I turned around and fled back in the direction of the abbey. There might be hunters there, but I thought of the abbey as home. Besides, there might be hunters anywhere.

The hunters might be loyal to the warrior princess — but maybe they misunderstood her wishes.

I shuddered as I ran.

I opened my mouth and words came tumbling out:

"'I am compassionate, and I am cruel.
Be on your guard!'"

Chapter Seventeen

"Times are changing," said the Priest. His eyes tilted down at the outer edges. His shoulders drooped. He looked sad as he sat behind his desk. He always looked sad. But there was something different about him today.

Despite his perpetual sadness, my teacher hummed a little tune under his breath. His skin looked dewy. His sparse hair was disheveled. In the top back of his head, a wisp stood straight up like a little flag that had been planted there. He seemed distracted and a little pleased with himself. I wondered if it had anything to do with Thomas. When I had been walking to the Priest's office, I had seen Thomas walking down the hall in the opposite direction. He may have been coming from the Priest's office. When he saw me, he turned away, quickened his step, and went down one of the side corridors.

I sat in my usual chair opposite my teacher. I noticed a new stack of papers and books facing the front of his desk. The books looked modern. The pages were ragged, but the edges were brighter than those of older books. I suspected that these books were mass produced rather than hand copied by the monks.

I wanted to ask what the books were — or at least what subjects they contained. But before I could ask, the Priest continued talking.

"The last Holy War I heard about was in the late 1300s when the Christian Cypriots established an outpost to fight the Muslim Turks…" he was thoughtful for a moment. "There was so much commercial interest in the wars, that I don't know why scholars called it them 'Holy Wars.'"

Holy War? It seemed like a contradiction in terms. Then I remembered that I had heard the term used before — when my father would say Christendom was expanding thanks to the "Holy Wars." It seemed like he should have been proud of this. But he always had bitterness in his voice and usually mentioned that entire generations of men had died in the same families. Once he mentioned that a distant part of our family had been murdered by men who were on their way to distant lands in the name of a "Holy War." The cousins had been Christian peasants who lived in the far edge of our Kingdom. They spoke a different dialect than those who slaughtered them. My father said bitterly that the Pope had given those who went to war license to unleash the monsters within and become murders.

There was nothing holy about murder.

My mother had always shushed my father when she found me within earshot. Once I heard her telling my father that such talk was not for my innocent ears. My father replied that I would become a man soon enough and that I should know the ways of men. My mother had replied that there would be time enough for that.

My mother only told me about one "Holy War." I still remember her taking me in her lap, and telling me that a few hundred years ago, in the early 1200s, a group of young adults and children decided to spread the righteous cause of Christendom. They believed their innocence would allow them to succeed where their elders had failed. Then my mother told me that their innocence had not protected them. They had disappeared.

Rumor had it that they had been slaughtered or sold into slavery. Then my mother made me solemnly swear that I never leave the house without telling her where I was going.

"I heard about the 'Holy Wars' but I never formally learned about them," I told the Priest.

He gazed at me levelly in silence.

"Monks are only taught what they need to know," he slowly replied.

I bristled inwardly. I did my best not to sound defensive. But I wanted to let him know that my earliest education was at the knee of my mother and that it did not begin in a school or monastery.

"But my mother did tell me about the children who were slaughtered when they marched to a 'Holy War' in distant lands," I said.

"Oh, hogwash," the Priest said. He was so irritated that the air around him seemed to fold in on itself. "That's never been proven. I'm sure it's just an old wives' tale."

I must have looked crestfallen. I really did miss my mother and I didn't appreciate the Priest dismissing what she had told me. Monks weren't allowed to leave the abbey and we couldn't have visitors, so I never saw her. My mother must not have known about this when she encouraged my desire to be a monk and live in the abbey.

"It's natural that when you were a child that your mother would tell you a cautionary tale to protect you…"

I looked at him and wordlessly opened my mouth.

I gazed at the Priest in wonder. I hadn't told him that my mother made me swear that I would never leave the house and I wondered how he knew she was trying to protect me.

I was pleading with my eyes that he not besmirch the memory of my mother. I hadn't seen my mother in the four years that I had left home to live in the abbey and become a monk. There were strong rules about not leaving the abbey walls — even to visit family — and against family members coming to visit. My mother was getting older when I left. Her knee hurt so badly that she walked with a cane. My last memory of her was of her leaning on her cane and waving goodbye to me with moist eyes.

"I'm sure that she believed what she told you was true," the Priest said softly. "And if it were true, God would have protected those children and awarded them a special place in heaven if any danger had befallen them."

"But still, the children's parents must have suffered," I answered.

"Yes, it would have been natural for their parents to have suffered," he continued – "IF the tale were true. As I mentioned, it probably wasn't true. And even so, remember that suffering is an important part of Christianity."

I looked at him blankly.

His sadness turned again to irritation.

"Must I go back to the beginning?"

I simply stared. I felt hazy today as if everything was happening under a layer of fog. Maybe I hadn't gotten enough sleep last night. I was tossing and turning all night and into the wee hours of the morning. Even now I felt the tug of betrayal. Strong emotion tugged at me. I felt like an hour glass with all the sands running out. It was as if by betraying my friend, the unicorn, I had betrayed myself.

"Christ died on the cross for our sins," stated the Priest crossly.

"If he died on the cross for our sins, then why must we suffer also?"

I had spoken without thinking. But it was an innocent enough question. I really was curious.

The Priest scowled.

"Life is full of suffering. To think that we could be free from all suffering, is naive. Because we suffer, we can appreciate it when we do not suffer," he replied.

I stopped for a moment to consider that not suffering was related to suffering.

"Are you saying then that we wouldn't know peace unless we knew suffering — just as there would be no heaven without hell?"

"Some people would say so," replied my teacher, nodding sagely. He dropped his sneer and smiled serenely.

I put my hand of the knee of my robe to stop my fingers from trembling. Next to the dark brown of my robe, my fingers were as pale as alabaster. I cursed my lack of sleep. Then I remembered why I had been tossing and turning. My conscience plagued me about the unicorn. Where was she? Was she alive or dead? Even if she were alive, then she was being hunted. And I was the cause of this. In the interest of getting ahead, I had betrayed her.

We were both suffering. This last thought gave me pause. I suffered because I betrayed a being who was pure and true. I suffered because of the deafening pangs of my conscience. But this proved that I had a conscience. I imagined that most who plotted to get ahead felt nothing but irritation if their plan went awry. But I felt guilty to the point where I suffered. I suffered so much that I felt exalted in my suffering.

"I understand!"

I couldn't stop myself from exclaiming. It was as if a bolt of lightning hit me. I was that electrified.

The Priest widened his eyes.

"I mean that I understand Christ suffering on the cross, because I am suffering. I understand now that Christ never meant that he suffered so that we would never suffer. He meant to show his example of suffering. He was suffering for us so that we could suffer for him and for each other."

"Perhaps." The Priest narrowed his eyes at me as he uttered his one-word reply.

We were both silent for a moment.

"And what are you suffering about?" The Priest broke the silence. His question seemed innocent enough, so I answered it without thinking.

"I betrayed an innocent creature — the unicorn. The Bishop told me that she would not be harmed, but who knows," I replied.

"Yes," said the Priest. He looked down at his desk and seemed distracted, but his words were precise. "One doesn't know. The hunters answer to the King, not to the Bishop."

I felt my shoulders collapse as my entire posture slumped forward. This was true. I had forgotten because we in the abbey looked to the Bishop as our absolute authority. But the hunters lived outside the abbey – even though they were within the abbey walls the day I had pointed out my unicorn to them.

"You see — your suffering is an illusion. You are suffering over something that is most probably a figment of your imagination." The Priest stared at me gloatingly.

"Are you saying that I made the creature up — that the unicorn is a figment of my imagination?"

I was incredulous.

"Yes. That is what I am saying."

"But I told you the unicorn is real. I can prove that she exists. You said yourself that once the hunters capture her and take her to the King, the Bishop and the King will always remember my name."

"Then again" — mused the Priest slowly — "perhaps you are right. Maybe the creature does exist. Just this morning when I was walking by the clearing, I saw…"

"What did you see? The unicorn? Is she okay? Remember — I saw her first. I am the one who is going be rewarded by the Bishop." I blurted out the words so rapidly that I didn't know if the Priest heard everything I said.

I felt my cheeks reddening. My ears tingled. I suspected they were turning red also. I was appalled by the words that had tumbled out of my mouth especially the last part of expecting to be rewarded by the Bishop. I felt like I had become an opportunist. I had started on this path and now I could not control what I was becoming.

"Relax. I was just going to say that I sensed a presence near the clearing. I thought of you and your mythical creature. But then when I turned my head, all I saw was a stand of birch trees."

I breathed more deeply and sat up.

"That's better," said the Priest. "I see that you are suffering — more than you should. Maybe it's all in your imagination — and perhaps your imagination is the will of God. But perhaps now that you have confessed wanting to be rewarded by the Bishop, you can start to feel better. We all want to be better than we are. It makes sense that you want to move ahead, especially since you are from humble origins. But remember what the Bible says in Matthew 5:5 – 'Blessed are the meek: for they shall inherit the earth.' This means that if you are content with your lot, you will be happier."

"You are right, father." I bowed my head humbly. I recognized that there was much wisdom in his words, but I also felt resentful. Who was he to tell me that I should be meek and accept my lot? He was a priest and, as such, he had authority.

I reminded myself that things loomed larger in my imagination. It was as if my mind played a game of shadow puppets with me. Things would work out. The unicorn would be okay. After all, it was unthinkable that anything would happen to her. I believed in God's will and I knew he would recognize my deservedness. But I also knew that I had to change the course of the conversation.

"But tell me, father: Why is it that God makes us suffer so. I am speaking of real suffering."

My teacher looked at me quizzically.

"Perhaps if you give me an example, it would help me answer."

"The Black Death, for example," I said in response. "The epidemic ended some time ago — but so many died, and the sickness was so bad — that to this day people still talk of it and fear it."

The Priest's eyes deepened and looked sadder. "Yes. It was hundreds of years ago. I remember the stories passed down to me that some distant cousins of mine had died in the plague around 1350. They were among the nearly half of the population who died from plague."

"Yes, many died. Mother told me that there were bodies strewn in the streets and wagons full of the dead were everywhere."

When I looked at my teacher, I saw that his eyes were moist.

I suddenly became aware that my eyes were moist also. For a moment, it felt as though my heart beat outside of my skin. I felt compassion for all those who had suffered from the plague — for those afflicted by the disease, for the families who lost their loved ones, even for the wagon drivers and their horses. The scene my mother had described truly was horrifying.

"She told me that the disease ridden were swollen and had purplish blotches. Then she told me that this was why I must always, always wash my hands, particularly before I eat.

The Priest smiled in a way that started to look like a sneer.

"That's as good of a cautionary tale as any," he said. "But dirty hands never caused the plague. Most people blamed the Jews."

"The Jews!?" I was incredulous. I couldn't believe my teacher thought this. "I never heard such a thing," I added. "I heard the plague was spread by rats arriving from distant lands in the holds of ships."

"I heard that too. But I always thought it sounded more plausible that God was angered by the Jews. They lived in some of the cities then — in the ghettoes, of course, with their own kind. God must have been angered because of the Jew's proximity to Christians. The leaders of some of the cities threw them out. But it was too late. The plague had already spread."

"But sir, that's not logical. When I was a boy, we knew some Jewish merchants who came through the village. They didn't talk about being Jewish, of course, but we could tell by the yellow badges that they were required to wear. They were upstanding people. My mother said some were quite intelligent."

The Priest narrowed his eyes. "Some Jews are too intelligent. I hear that some of them teach in the religious studies departments in the universities in Paris. With the mass production of books, too many people are reading, and they think they are figuring things out for themselves. If we're not careful, most people will think they don't need the Church anymore."

I looked at him wordlessly. I really didn't know what to say.

"I hear they have mass produced a Bible in Germany," he continued. "Soon they'll be printing them in other languages.

It was better when the Bible was forbidden to everyone except for the clergy."

The Priest looked somewhat embarrassed, as if he had said too much. "Besides, logic has nothing to do with it," he spat. "God's will is arbitrary — not logical."

"But the philosophers taught us that things should make sense — that we should ask questions of the world around us," I blurted.

"You mean the *pagan* philosophers," he countered. "Aristotle and Plato were not Christians — they were pagan. They had no belief in God's will."

"But they had fate," I argued. "Sometimes when things happen for no reason, we still call it fate. But here, in the abbey, we are more likely to call it God's will. Perhaps it is really the same thing."

"It is NOT the same thing," countered the Priest. "God's will is pre-ordained. It is pre-destination."

"Father, you know best," I said lowering my eyes. "You are right about most things — including God's will. But I take exception to blaming the plague on the Jews. As I mentioned, I have known a few and they are upstanding people."

The Priest took a deep breath and seemed to relax as he looked at me.

"Perhaps you are right. It's just that I heard the others blame the Jews and I went along with them, so they wouldn't look at me suspiciously. Maybe it *was* the rats that caused the plague. Perhaps in years to come, men will figure what caused the plague and then it will never happen again…"

Almost as an afterthought, he added, "But when it comes to suffering of that magnitude, God is trying to teach us something."

"Of course, He is," I answered.

I felt emboldened by the peace between us. I had influenced my teacher's thoughts much as he had molded mine. I should have left well enough alone.

"At least now I know the answer," I said.

"The answer to what?"

"To what heresy is all about — you know the question that I asked a while ago. You just mentioned that you were afraid that people would start looking to themselves for their spiritual sustenance — that they eventually might not need the Church."

"I mentioned that people might *think* they don't need the church, but they are wrong," countered the Priest. "They will always need us. The Jews are part of this. That's why I reconsidered the belief that I long held. Saint Augustine said it best. He believed that the Jews were necessary because their religion gave Christianity its history."

I nodded.

"That's true," I said, "but it doesn't explain why when people have their own beliefs, the Church calls it heresy, and anyone who doesn't agree with them is burned at the stake."

"That's a myth that people are burned at the stake," countered the Priest.

We locked eyes. We both knew that it wasn't a myth, but he was my teacher, so I remained silent.

"But there are heretics. And when people don't agree with us — when they insist on clinging to their old ways as in the case of the pagans or the followers of the so-called 'Goddess'–cults — they *are* heretics. They threaten our way of life, so they must be dealt with."

I looked at the Priest and said nothing. All I could think of was my beloved unicorn. I had betrayed her. What was going to become of her? I was truly suffering.

Chapter Eighteen

"'In the beginning was the Word, and the Word was with God, and God was the Word.'"

I studied the Greek words in the Bible that I had placed on the olden wooden desk before me — lingering over the word *logos*. The page was old and brittle so I traced my index finger in the air over the long lines of the *lambda*, the circle of the *omicron*, the crevice of the *gamma*, the roundness of the second *omicron* and the plural *sigma* at the end that looked like a curved snake with its head below the bottom line.

There was a long narrow gold and blue "J" travelling the length of the page on the left-hand side of the page. It looked like a spear but on closer inspection, I could see that it was an elongated and elaborate letter. This was the first page of the Gospel of John in The New Testament.

I felt my eyes widen as I thought about the fact that I just happened to flip open to this page. I had long had a love of language, reading and writing. The Bible fell open to the perfect page for me. I took it as a sign. This was a special Bible. It was in Greek rather than the Latin Bibles that the priests used in the abbey. This Bible looked old and valuable.

I had found it in the back of the shelf hidden away behind the more modern books. I wondered who had stashed it there and why.

The word for God — *Theos* —was there too. It was one of the first Greek words that I had memorized. I located the first *Theos* and traced my finger in the air over the capitalized *theta* that was narrow and elongated, a large "O" with a horizontal line through it; followed by a small *epsilon* like the Latin "*e*" but curved; the *omicron*, and the plural *sigma*. As important as this word was, it felt secondary.

Logos seemed to be the most important word. From listening to the Priest, I knew the "Word" was supposed to be Jesus. God sent his only son, Jesus, to earth to spread his teachings. So, the story went. But "word" was the subject of the first clause – so even grammatically it was the main event. The sentence mentioned God — but it did not mention his son, Jesus. That was something the Priest said. Everybody was just supposed to accept it. *Why did the Priest have so much power? Why did I want that power?*

"'In beginning was the Word, and the Word was with God, and God was the Word.'"

Because of the long illuminated initial, I almost thought that the book was a psaltery. But I didn't think a book of the psalms would also house the canonical gospels.

The book looked elaborate enough to have been used in a coronation. Who had used it?

What had they used it for?

The passage didn't make me think of Jesus. It seemed to be saying that the written word was sacred – maybe especially that the Greek word was sacred. It was, after all, the most ancient language that I understood — although there must have been others that came before. I shuddered, wondering what secrets the ancient languages would unlock.

For as far back as I could remember, I have always loved stories. I loved the worlds they created, and I loved that those worlds lived in my head. (I also loved my mother's soft voice, the brush of her lips on my forehead at bedtime before I fell asleep.) When I learned to read and write, I was amazed to see the letters that I wrote forming sounds and then words.

To me, the word was always sacred. The word was how ideas were expressed. The word represented thought. It was the word that drove me to see the world more brightly. The word could change hearts and minds. The word was everything.

I imagined how scholars deciphered languages. Maybe they found the languages that went before the languages they were studying. Perhaps they looked for similar characters and patterns of word endings. Perhaps they discovered how the language flowed by looking at the white space — or the empty beige clay of the tablets at the end of the line. Maybe there was an ancient stone hidden somewhere — that would tell them, for instance, the meaning of the Egyptian hieroglyphs. Maybe someday they would find this key.

Maybe they would tell of sacred creatures who were rarely seen by humans. Maybe these creatures had their own language.

I looked around the library guiltily. If there was anyone there, they might be able to read my heretical thoughts.

I was still thinking of Thomas after seeing him walk down the hall from my teacher's office yesterday.

I doubted that I would see him — or for that matter Gregory — in the library. Gregory would just have been here last time because he was looking for a secluded place to express his sorrow. And Thomas — if he was romantically involved with Father Matthew — would have no need to come to the library.

They were young men who loved themselves more than musty old books. They certainly didn't love their sad and weary teacher even if they pretended that they did.

I guessed that most people loved themselves first.

I had myself to look at. I had loved my beloved unicorn — and I betrayed her for my own gain.

I had even come to the library for myself.

When I was learning ancient Greek, I always felt reassured. The language made me think of my mother and the stories she used to tell me.

She didn't speak Greek, of course. She always spoke in her peasant French. But she told me many of the Greek myths and legends that she had learned from her father. One of my favorite stories was about Jason and the Argonauts searching for their fabled Golden Fleece.

I would close my eyes at bedtime when my mother told me the story of Jason. He learned that to return to his native land and become King, he must first bring back the fleece of the Golden Ram which was located on a far-away island. With the help of the god and goddesses, especially his special goddess, Hera, he chose his crew. They assembled a wooden boat and embarked on the first long-distance ocean voyage. The fleece hung on a tree on the island of Colchis, then on the edge of the known world. The fleece was hung by the son of *Helios*, the sun god, in a sacred grove, and it was guarded by bulls and a magical dragon who never slept.

To get to the island, the ship — steered by Jason — and rowed by his Argonauts, his crew of sailors, the men had to forge unknown territories of the sea which included treacherous islands.

Every night, my mother would tell me of their harrowing adventures, that included visiting an island with towering, life-threatening giants. At the very end of the story, before Jason and the Argonauts reached their destination, they had to pass through the clashing rocks that guarded the entrance to the Black Sea. I do not remember the ending — only that Jason did reach his destination and found the Golden Fleece. I imagined that when they were traveling the sea at night they looked up and guided themselves with the constellation of Aries which is Latin for Ram.

My mother did not turn the pages of the book and read to me because there was no book. She didn't know how to read because it was forbidden for women to be educated. So, she just told me the story from her memory – of how it was told to her.

Many years later when I entered the monastery, the Priest told me that the Golden Fleece represented many things, chief among them the forgiveness of God. He then went on to tell me, with great authority, that "the heroic character of Jason was a re-invention of Jesus." When I innocently asked how Jason could be a reinvention of Jesus, when the tale of *Jason and the Argonauts* was written so long ago, the Priest just gave me a blank look.

I gazed at a ray of sun filtering down from a high window in the dusty library and wondered briefly if there was any connection between the Golden Fleece and the Holy Grail. Both were brilliant and gleaming like the sunlight.

I looked down at the Greek New Testament still open on the desk before me. I didn't know enough Greek to understand all the words on the page — but I did know the Greek word for light: *phos*. Again, and again, my eyes came back to it. I knew what the lines said because I had studied the Bible in Latin. The lines in the Gospel of John had caught my eye: "'The same came for a witness, to bear witness of the Light, that all *men* through Him might believe; He was not that Light, but *was sent* to bear witness of that Light; *That* was the true Light, which lighteth every man that cometh into the world.'"

I studied the lines of the opening Greek character Phi. It looked like an upside-down pitchfork with curved prongs. This was followed by a lowercase *omega* — pronounced like the Latin O — and ended in the plural *sigma* which was a Latin *c* sitting on the line and lowering to the left in a curving subscript. I said the word softly under my breath: *phos.*

The word made me think of the brightest light I had ever seen when I was a young monk and had glimpsed my beloved unicorn in the clearing. It seemed like the sun was blazing into the unicorn's magical horn and her white body. The light behind her was magnified by the stands of white birch trees.

Perhaps we are all creatures of the light.

Like Jason and like the knights of King Arthur's Round Table — who searched for the Holy Grail — I felt that I, too, had something bright and gleaming in my future.

Chapter Nineteen

After I left the library, I went for a walk through the center of the grounds toward the East wall. I loved books, but I loved nature too. I needed to clear my mind. The grass, the trees, the blue sky, the white wisps of clouds all smiled around me. A few birds chirped. I could hear their feathered throats pulsating. Their calls sounded like music.

Nature was in her glory. The feast day of Pentecost, and its "kneeling prayer" was already three weeks behind us. Time was passing quickly — shedding its beauty in petals from flowering trees. Pink and white and every shade in between showered down in the abbey.

I slowed my step when I neared the clearing. I hadn't thought about where I was going, but now I knew. I wanted to find my beloved unicorn. I needed to somehow tell her that she was in danger. Most of all I desired to say that I was sorry. I looked up at the blue sky, folded my hands palm to palm and held them up. I prayed to God in the heavens that I might see my beloved unicorn and that she could somehow understand me.

I closed my eyes. I wondered if I were praying for too many things. Maybe it was too much to pray to see the unicorn AND to be able to talk to her. Perhaps I should just pray to see her and take care of the rest myself. Maybe asking for both things was asking too much of God. But what if I only prayed to see her and then I did see her but then I couldn't communicate with her. Then my prayer to God would be useless and I would be wasting His time. My doubt passed. I decided it was okay to pray for two things especially if they were related to each other.

I prayed into a long tunnel of sky that reached the heavens. I felt the sun enter my bones.

Dear Heavenly Father, I said silently. *I know that I have sinned. I have put my beloved unicorn above all others. I hope you can forgive me – but I feel only holiness when I think of her. She is the holder of all things bright and good to me. She is the chalice that I drink from. No injury is meant to you and your son .... and the holy ghost, I added* (even though I didn't fully understand that yet). *I am coming to you because I betrayed her, all that is good, for my own gain. I wish to undo that. I wish to tell her that she is in danger and that I will do anything to help her. I would even offer my life instead of hers.*

That last part about offering my life instead of hers just kind of slipped in. But it was true. I was willing to die for her. I had never felt so valiant.

When I opened my eyes, I was surprised at what I saw – but I did not see my unicorn.

A man in a pointed cap, green like the rest of his outfit, was pointing an arrow at me.

I had dropped my hands from the position of prayer. They hung in their normal place at my sides. But I quickly held them up in the air and I opened my palms in the gesture of peace.

"I am a friend," I said. "I am unarmed and open minded." As I spoke, I examined the man. At first, he seemed boyish because of his thin build and sprightly dress. But under his green cap I saw a face that was wizened and aged. He had a bulbous red-veined nose. With the red and green, I wondered for a moment if he were an apparition — a holly bush that had shape shifted into an elf.

"You are dressed like a monk — are you a monk? And it looked like you were praying. Were you? Never mind, it doesn't matter. Everyone knows that the clergy is corrupt. I am Robin Hood and I am here to protect the poor."

The man then pulled back his arm that was holding the bow.

I thought fast. The man standing in front of me was most definitely not an apparition. And he was not an elf. He was human. I could tell from his guttural voice. He couldn't be the real Robin Hood, of course. Robin Hood existed more than a few centuries ago in a land far from here. But I heard that the character of Robin Hood a few years back was the star in a play staged in a village not far from here. The man probably was rewarded for his persona by tavern keepers who gave him free drinks. Maybe, at this point, he really did think he was Robin Hood. Who knew?

I thought fast.

"Wait! We are not unalike sire," I said. "I became a monk because I wanted to do good. I never feel the presence of God more than when I am giving alms to the poor."

This was not entirely true. I never felt the presence of God more than when I was gazing raptly at my beloved unicorn. I also felt the presence of God in nature. But I also felt close to God when giving alms to the poor.

It wasn't that I felt better about myself in the presence of the poor because I was not among them. I knew this motivated many. I was different. True, I knew where my next meal was coming from. But I had taken a vow of poverty. I could own no land, no jewels, nothing. I felt the presence of God, because I was helping his children. The first time I gave a gaunt starving woman dressed in rags, what was probably the only meal she had in days, I understood the Bible passage — "the meek shall inherit the earth."

The meek were the only righteous people because they did not scheme to get ahead. They were mostly content with their lot — just as the Priest had told me. They were simple and humble. They were grateful when they received help.

The Robin Hood imposter must have sensed that I was sincere in what I said. He relaxed his arm and put his bow over his arm and the arrow back in his quiver.

"I was searching for the great cathedral at Notre Dame, but now that I look around ... this place reminds me more of the abbey at Nottingham," he said. "I believe that you are a good and humble monk. But where there is religion, there is money. The Church takes it from the poor in their mandatory tithes and in the collection plates from the common folk.

I am Robin Hood and I intend to take the money back —and give it to the poor."

I saw an opportunity here to be rid of this man.

"The Bishop is scheduled to hold a special council tonight before vespers at the church. He has a ruby ring with a gold band, and I hear he has a miniature sundial on his wristband." I pointed toward the church.

"A sundial wristband?" asked the Robin Hood imposter. "That's all the rage now. I bet that'll fetch a pretty penny."

I nodded solemnly. I doubted that any money that he robbed from the Bishop or from anyone for that matter would make it to the poor. I had heard that all thieves were called Robin Hood. I suspected that the thief was just going to fill his own belly. It was also possible that if I saw the imposter again, he would be wearing the sundial wristband.

The man turned in the direction of the church. Suddenly, I felt emboldened. I had once bowed my head to the Bishop, but no more. If any harm befell him from this almost comical imposter of Robin Hood, it was not my fault. Maybe this was God's way of answering my prayers. Perhaps whatever befell the Bishop, would help my beloved unicorn.

If any harm came to him, it was God's will.

As I meandered through the abbey, continuing my walk, I stopped to examine a leaf on the branch of a tree. The leaf had twelve lobes. It was a multiplication of two of the hexagonal six-sided pattern that appeared so often in nature. This reminded me of the poetic hexameter. Even language took on the forms of nature.

The leaf was shiny green and dark and had a spine down the center. Other lines — like the veins in my hand — led from the center toward each lobe. I wondered if the spine down the center had the same purpose as the human spine. I wondered how the tree knew to grow leaves that all had the same hexagonal design. Nature must have a divine plan. I knew that if I told the Priest, he would say that this was heretical thinking. Although for the first time, I really didn't care what the Priest thought. I couldn't help what I thought. Maybe God put the thoughts in my mind.

I almost laughed out loud. But at the last minute, I stopped myself.

There was a hush in the abbey, and I wanted to respect that. I was approaching the East wall of the grounds where the hush was particularly profound since it was the area where the silent nuns lived.

I was still hoping to see my beloved unicorn, of course. I always was – even when I wouldn't admit it to myself. But I felt like if God wanted me to see her I would.

It was God's will — and it was out of my hands.

Suddenly I felt freer.

I walked on for a while and then I heard whispers. They sounded female. I hid behind a wide and tall holly bush and saw the two nuns that I had seen before.

"Here Kitty, Kitty," said one.

I could only see the bottom of her white habit, but she paused. I had the distinct impression that she was looking around.

"Forget about Kitty for one moment," said the one with the higher voice.

"But she might need me," responded the nun with the lower voice. I brought a pail with some water in it. I was going to bring milk, but I was afraid that it would cause suspicion if word got out that I was taking things from the larder."

"Stealing," replied the one with the higher voice. "You would be stealing from the larder if you brought milk for Kitty, and stealing is a sin."

Stealing *was* a sin and that was serious. But the nun with the higher voice sounded like she was on the verge of a giggle.

"It's not a sin if I use the milk to feed one of God's creatures," responded the nun with the lower voice.

"But is Kitty one of God's creatures?" The one with the higher voice spoke tauntingly. "Mother Superior wouldn't say so. It's no secret how she feels about cats."

"Her — and most of Christendom. I know. I know," replied the one with the lower voice. "But Kitty is not a representative of Satan. She's got beautiful light gray stripes against a darker gray background. And the white hair on her nose accentuates her pink nostrils. I was noticing how beautiful she was just the other day when she let me gaze at her for a long time."

I heard the nun with the higher voice sigh.

"Kitty is clean. She licks herself all the time just like all cats do," said the one with the lower voice. "Not to mention that if more cats were allowed to live it would help to eliminate or at least reduce the mice and rat populations. Maybe we'd have less sickness. Cats are natural predators. I watched Kitty tracking a chipmunk for more than an hour the other day."

The other nun sighed again and resignedly said, "Oh, you and that cat."

Then she changed her tone and said, "but that's one of the things that I love about you — your devotion. When you love someone or … something … you are relentless with your love."

"Kitty is hardly 'something,'" responded the other nun sullenly.

"That's true. I didn't mean to insult her," replied the one with the soprano voice.

"That's right, Kitty is very special. Today she led me to you," said the woman with the lower voice. I came outside because I was worried about her."

"That's true. It is good that we are finally together," replied the other. "We haven't seen each other alone for a while."

I shifted so that I had a better view.

"I tried to stay away from you, but it was very hard." The shorter one with the deeper voice was speaking.

"My darling, Isabella. I knew something was wrong when I waited and waited for you and you never came. You can always tell me what you are feeling," replied the taller one with the higher voice.

"I was in such agony, staying away from you, Heloise," confided Isabella. "I knew the Mother Superior was on to us and I didn't want to make her even more angry."

"I told you there is no pleasing the Mother Superior. She's always angry. I think she was born that way." Heloise giggled.

"Sshh," Isabella admonished. "Someone might hear you. We are not allowed to talk in the abbey."

"We are not allowed to talk anywhere," retorted Heloise. If she sang in the choir — if women were *allowed* in the choir — her voice would be as pure as any eunuch.

"To tell you the truth," whispered Isabella, "I thought she was right. I thought loving you was an abomination in the eyes of God. But I suffered so much trying to stay away from you. God would never want me to be so miserable."

Heloise was quiet for a moment. Then she spoke:

"I thought you were trying to do what you thought was the right thing. That's why I didn't come after you. I wanted you to make up your own mind. But I wondered if you really love me. Do you, Isabella? Do you love me as much as I love you?"

"My God, YES. I love you more than the sky and the earth — more than the known lands and even more than the unknown lands. I love you so much I would die for you."

I remembered my prayer to God of wanting to die in the place of my beloved unicorn. Being willing to die for someone must be an expression of love — though in my case the love I feel for the unicorn is chaste. But I had a feeling that with these two women, being willing to die for love might not be just an expression.

Chapter Twenty

I circled back from the grove near the castle where I thought I would find the warrior princess jousting with the other maidens. Instead, I had seen a future that terrified me. It was the same scene that the ex-nun — now a young wife — who had escaped the abbey had been weaving on the loom in her cottage in the woods. It was me — or a creature who strongly resembled me — sitting inside a fence and I — or the image of one who looked like me — was wearing a collar chained to a tree.

I had to get back to the abbey. I knew there might be hunters there, but they might be anywhere. I felt safe in the abbey. When I look back now, I see that it would have been better if I had wandered the land rather than calling one area home and then returning to it. I jumped high with all my strength and flew back over the abbey wall.

When I reached the middle of the abbey grounds, I found myself surrounded by hunters and their hounds. I did not want to hurt anyone, but I had no choice. I had to defend myself.

When I kicked backwards from my hindquarters and hit the hunter behind me, it felt like I was hurting myself. Certainly, when I stabbed my horn into the side of the hound who was lunging at me, I felt bad. People think that the horn makes us fierce warriors or that our horns are magical, but I have a different theory. The horn is to make us beautiful. It also makes us unique. To be unique is to be beautiful.

The horn is NOT for stabbing hounds.

But a loud voice in my head told me that to escape, I had to defend myself.

I noticed that the hound was bleeding, and I could not bear to look so I quickly turned my head. I saw a movement behind a tree to the side of the hunters. Someone was hiding there. At first, I thought that it was another hunter waiting to join the ambush. Then I saw one eye and then another. One eye was bigger than the other. A man's face popped out from behind the tree. He wore a brown robe. For a few seconds I locked eyes with the man. It was my young friend.

Surely, he would save me, I thought. In those days I always thought that someone would come along and save me — the warrior princess, my young man. With age, I realize that I have to save myself.

I stared at him. He looked terrified and slunk back behind the tree.

I opened my mouth and chanted:
"And do not banish me from your sight.
And do not make your voice hate me, nor your hearing.

. . . .

I am the silence that is incomprehensible
*   and the idea whose remembrance is frequent.*
I am the voice whose sound is manifold
*   and the word whose appearance is multiple.*

. . . .

"'For I am knowledge and ignorance.
I am shame and boldness.
I am shameless; I am ashamed.
I am strength and I am fear.'"

I did not know where the words came from but when I uttered them, I felt free. The hunter closest to me, wearing a belted burgundy robe and a tan wide brimmed hat, looked at me aghast as if he had never seen a talking unicorn before. Then I fled and left the hunters behind me in a cloud of dust.

It did not matter that the blue sky above me had never known smokestacks. The hunters had been suffocating me. I could smell them, and their stench was impure.

It did not matter that the princess had not come to my rescue (*yet*, I remember thinking).

I fled toward the purest scent I know — that of a maiden.

Chapter Twenty-One

As I was running, I thought to myself – *now where would a maiden be?* I thought of the cloister in the abbey — with the silent nuns — but then thought better of it.

Chances were that I would find a virginal maiden there, but odds were good that she would be so afraid that she would report me to the Bishop.

Now, looking back, I see that in my rational mind, I would have known that I had to save myself. But in my panic, with the hunters and their hounds so close behind me, I wanted to find a maiden who would save me. I was still looking for someone to rescue me so, obviously, I wasn't thinking straight. In my defense, I was very afraid.

I wanted to get as far away from the hunters as I could — so I simply fled. I was so frenzied that I didn't know what direction I was going in. Then, as I galloped toward the West wall, I realized that I was retracing my steps.

I jumped over the wall and as I did, I felt a sense of freedom. The hunters were safely behind me, and the abbey wall was between us. Now that I've had time to reflect on the situation, I'm painfully aware that the hunters could have found a way to pass over or through the wall also. Maybe they even knew of an opening somewhere.

I've been thinking that it's very likely that my capture was all part of a plan that involved the tapestry maker as well as the hunters. When I had stood in the clearing and stared into the window of the little house where I had seen my image being woven into the round wooden pen, I never imagined that the young wife might be trying to ensnare me. But now I have a strong sense that she was involved. She wove a supposed reality that was designed to bring me to an end.

In a way, she was participating with the hunters, and probably the Bishop and who knows who else — maybe the King and the Warrior Princess also if my suspicions were true and the Princess wanted me for a pet. Sometimes desire can create reality. You might desire something so strongly that it comes true and by the time you get what you desire, then you may find that it is too late to change your mind. Then there you are —seemingly against your will — at a new place in your life.

Sometimes the mind can create reality. Between the young wife who had woven my image into the fenced-in pen and my own non-rational mind that still expected that someone would rescue me, my fate may have been sealed already.

I see now that I would have been better off had I hid in the forest. I could have sustained myself by feeding off the wild plants and drinking from the dark springs of gurgling water. I could've told the difference between the plants — those that were edible and those that were poisonous — with my sense of smell that would have become heightened in the dark. There would have been no bright shafts of sun, no small ponds in which to see my reflection. But I would have been able to smell and hear the water and in that way find what I needed.

Instead of asking for my help in purifying a stream so they could drink, any other animals, that I encountered in the woods, could have helped me. All I would have had to do was to swallow my pride and ask. I see that now, but at the time I never thought of it. It was, in fact, unthinkable that I should be the one who needed help.

Just because I am alone all the time, doesn't mean that I am not influenced by the world around me. I am vain. It has always been my nature. I know that now. Vain people do not ask for help. They give assistance to others. It is part of vanity to help others.

All I knew is that I had to get away from the hunters — far away. And to me, at that time, that meant putting the abbey wall between us. It felt like security then, but I see now that it meant nothing. In fact, it has just occurred to me that I may have walked into a trap that the hunters and their conspirators had set for me.

I went on my way — slowing down and occasionally sniffing the wild sage and clary with the tiny purple petals that grew at my feet. I was headed toward the castle. Surely, I would find a maiden near there. I was still exhausted from being ambushed and frightened so badly by the hunters and their hounds. At least I was no longer trembling. I wanted so badly just to lie down and sleep. But I knew that I couldn't do that.

I was used to hiding from people. But even now with the hunters still in the abbey — as far as I knew — on my scent, I had another reason to fear humans. I ambled along and even though I was exhausted, I tried to be as alert as possible by imaging that my horn could sense a maiden in my near future. It worked. I felt that my horn was leading me away from danger and toward goodness. I imagined that my horn was lighting the way.

As I wandered, I looked at the gently sloping hills in the distance. They were sprouting that vibrant yellow green of spring that means that everything is new and beautiful. Above the hills, the sky was a clear blue — the kind of azure sky that makes the expanse look wider than it is. My eyes wandered to the forest that I was walking next to. I looked up and saw a canopy of forest green leaves hanging above me to my right. Dappled light fell on the grass and the stubbly brush under my feet. The trees I walked between were low and sparse. They looked like they had grown from seedlings that had dropped from the tall trees edging the forest. The forest beside me was dense, endlessly dark. Aside from not wanting to get lost — I didn't even entertain the notion of enlisting the help of other animals — I didn't enter the forest because I shuddered at the thought of ending up at the clearing where I had seen the little house before. I winced at the memory of seeing the weaving of the image of the one who looked like me chained to a tree in the wooden pen.

By walking along the edge of the forest, I could just duck in if a human appeared and I needed to hide. But I hadn't seen any humans since I fled from the hunters. I knew I could make better time in the meadow next to the forest. It was morning when the hunters had ambushed me and not that much time had lapsed. When I looked ahead into the distance, I saw mist gathered over small green hills. The mist had settled into a low-lying valley. Higher up on the hills where the rays of the sun shone down, the mist slowly dissipated. As the yellow rays of the sun bore down and burnt the day into existence, I could see the curtain of mist vanish before my very eyes. The world was very beautiful. Maybe I sensed it would be over for me soon, but for whatever reason I felt that the beauty in front of me was terrifying. I trembled all the way down to my hooves.

I was still going in the direction of the castle. I intended to avoid the grove where the warrior princess used to joust with her handmaidens. This was the same clearing where, on my last visit, I had seen "my" wooden pen and the empty collar mirroring the scene being woven on the tapestry.

If the warrior princess wouldn't save me, then perhaps another maiden would.

Chapter Twenty-Two

"Now if I were a unicorn where would I be?" I muttered as I wandered the grounds of the abbey. I had to tell her that she was in danger. I had to apologize to her for my betrayal.

If only, I could find her. It occurred to me briefly that she might have left the abbey. But then I dismissed the thought. The abbey was the most quiet and peaceful place I had ever been. When I took my vows as a monk, I had to swear never to leave the abbey and not to see any visitors — including family. It was hard to imagine that I would never see my mother again. I hated the thought of her suffering because she could not see me again. But she would be comforted by the fact that I was safe in the abbey. And I had my memories. The priests were right to forbid us to leave the abbey. For there is much sin outside the walls of the abbey — including badly behaved men in taverns and wanton women selling their wares in cemeteries.

Everyone knew that battles rarely occurred in abbeys. Even though there were wild animals here, it was rare to see a hunting party gathered in the abbey. The hunters that gathered to find the unicorn — after I had spoken to the Bishop — may have been the first. I felt very guilty. But the other monks and priests were vying to get ahead. It wasn't a sin to want to be like the others. Or was it?

Suddenly, I thought, *If I were a bird or another unicorn, I would know.* That reminded me of the old stories that I had loved. Every night my mother would lull me to sleep with a Greek myth. She told me never to repeat them. Her father, who died when she was young, had told her the stories. But he had always warned her not to tell anyone because the priests said they came from "a dangerous book."

I agreed with my mother. We loved the old myths because they gave meaning to our lives. My memory of the stories still served me. I imagined myself growing a long white nose and a horse's head. I imagined myself with short white fur. I concentrated until it felt like a long, conical horn grew from in between my ears just above my forehead. I felt the heaviness of my horse body. I felt smooth strands against my back when I flicked my tail. I felt the solidness of my hooves against the new grass on the ground. My fantasy was so real that I felt an errant stiff white hair tickling my large, dark nostril in my white nose.

Without thinking, I rubbed my finger across the base of my nose — my *human* nose. I was going to look down and see if the bottom of me — at least — had changed into a unicorn's legs and hooves, but just then I was distracted by a flock of birds flying in the formation of a "V" across the sky.

If I were in one of the old myths, a Goddess would hear my prayers and turn me into a bird. I would spread my wings and flit from tree to tree and look down over the land until I found my beloved unicorn.

The birds flew away. I watched until the sky was empty of both the sight of them and the sound of their chirps. Then I looked down at my human body in my customary brown robe. I believed in magic. But I doubted there was a spell that could free me from my human body. Humans have caused so much suffering — just being one of them means that I shoulder part of the responsibility. I had joined the monks so that I could live with a pure heart. But look what I had done — I had betrayed my beloved unicorn.

I felt so bad that I decided to pray to God again.

I folded my hands together and began:

Dear Heavenly Father,

I come to you with great remorse. I have betrayed my beloved unicorn – the gentlest and purest creature who has ever lived. I betrayed her for my own gain. I betrayed her for the sin of Pride. I want to find her and somehow warn her.

The unicorn is the purest creature that I have ever met. She has an innocent heart and wishes no harm to befall anyone. All she wishes for is to be left to herself so that she can be allowed to exist and to continue to beautify your kingdom. Surely, she is proof that you exist.

Amen

I kept my eyes closed tightly when I finished. It occurred to me that the second part of my prayer could be used as a "doxology" — a short hymn in praise of God which could be added at the end of a psalm. I had just learned the word in my classical Greek studies. The first part was from *doxa* which meant "glory." And the second part of the word was from *logia* which meant "saying." When I first saw this, I realized that the second part, *logia*, must be related to *logos*, which means "word." With my eyes still shut, I considered the word in its Greek spelling. It began with the lowercase *delta* which was a slightly elongated circle ending with a slight curve at the

top, then the small "o" of the *omicron* followed by the curved
lines of an accented and lower-case *sigma* — which must be
pronounced like an "x" followed by another *omicron* and then
the sleek lines of a *lambda* which ended in an upside down "v"
with a slight curve at the end. This pointed to a third *omicron*
and then a lower-case *gamma* leading to the simple *iota* that
symbolized the Latin "i" and ending in the first letter of the
alphabet *alpha*. I repeated it to myself: *Doxologia.*

I opened my eyes and saw that everything looked the
same. I reached the clearing and looked in. The unicorn was
not there. How could it be that she was once there sitting in
the sun, looking like light, and now she was nowhere to be
found? I kept on walking.

The church and the short squat building that housed the
monks were behind me. I was walking toward the East end,
where the grass was taller. Deep purple violets dotted the green
grass at my feet. A stretch in front of me, a white morning
glory in full bloom entwined its way up a bush. Crimson centers nestled deep in white petals.

There were clumps of trees here and there. Dew sparkled.
Shafts of morning sun light fell through branches of trees. It
was so tranquil and beautiful that I forgot for a minute that
I was searching for my beloved unicorn. I stood still and ad-
mired the morning. I took a deep breath of air. It was so fresh
I could taste it. I drank it in. I exhaled beauty.

The scene in front of me was heavenly.

That reminded me of the prayer I had just said to God,
our Father in heaven. Of course, if the Priest heard it, he would
say that the unicorn was pagan. Or worse, he might scoff and
insist the unicorn was a figment of my imagination. But the
unicorn was real and so was the prayer. It was a doxology — a
short praise to God. I meant it when I said that the unicorn

was proof that God existed. The unicorn was goodness and light. She did not deserve conniving and bloodshed.

I shuddered to consider what I had participated in.

But then I rethought things. I only did it because I wanted to get ahead and so that people would listen to me. Of course, if I were to become a priest, I would lead them in the right direction — toward goodness. I would teach them to understand their own goodness and how to stay in that goodness and only act from there. By understanding themselves, they could direct their actions and be kind to each other. In this way, they would also be kind to themselves, because an injury to others is an injury to self. They could start by redirecting themselves. When they wanted to say a bad word, they would say something gracious. When they felt stingy, they could be generous. When they wanted to kill, they could love.

Wasn't that what it was all about?

But did wanting this in the future, justify my betrayal of the unicorn? I could forgive myself, but only to any extent. Guilt had prompted me to pray.

I didn't see the contradiction of believing the old myths and of praying to God the Father in heaven. They seemed like two sides of the same coin to me. If I could become a bird, I could fly closer to God. The ancients worshipped their own gods and goddesses. We, in the abbey, worshipped the one God. But He was still a god. I didn't think it was possible to have too many gods to pray too. I knew, though, that the priest would say otherwise. He would say that by me admitting that I worshipped more than one god — in addition to believing in the unicorn — I was confessing heresy. Perhaps he was right. I knew that the Church didn't condone my beliefs. I knew enough now to keep my thoughts to myself. This must be what the Priest meant when he said that the monks learn enough to know when to be silent. A warm breeze stroked my face, bringing me back to the present. There were consequences to being branded a heretic. Everyone knew that they could be burned alive, and so most said only what we were supposed to. But did this mean that we really believed? Perhaps with the threat of flames at our feet, we really were unable to believe — so preoccupied were we with saving our lives.

My mother believed in the old stories her father read to her, but if anyone had asked her, she would have denied it. She told me that her father had warned her that the priests told him that the myths came from "a dangerous book." My Latin teacher, whom I respected, was a "sodomite." But he would never tell anyone. The young nun who fell in love with the carpenter and fled the abbey to live with him was now most likely an outcast. The two nuns who I had seen in the abbey seemed to love each other in a way that I might not ever understand. I had seen my beloved unicorn more than several times now and I knew that she was real. But I knew I did not love her the way the two nuns loved each other.

In my mind, their love — even though it was different, or maybe *because* it was different — seemed more real to me that the paintings that hung in the church — the images that were supposed to represent "belief."

I started walking in the direction of the East wall of the abbey and passed a sturdy oak tree that had a trunk slightly larger than the width of a man. I remembered now that I had intended on protecting my beloved unicorn the last time, I had seen her. Some days ago, I had been out walking and had spotted the hunters in the distance. They were stalking something. When I looked closer and saw white hindquarters, I gasped.

I had quickened my step and hid behind a tree trunk. I intended to pop out and startle the hunters, so my beloved unicorn could run away. But when I looked out from behind the tree trunk, I found that I was closer to the hunters than I thought. Then I looked ahead of the hunters at my beloved unicorn. Just at that moment, she had turned her head in my direction. I was going to yell. Instead, I found myself terrified and trembling. I was so close to the hunters. What if they found me and killed me? It would be easy enough. There had been no other witnesses around. It would have been easy enough for them to say it was an accident. I slunk back behind the tree-trunk. My beloved unicorn must have thought me a coward. I was going to come to her rescue, but then I did nothing.

I recalled that I had felt terrible then. I still felt horrible.

Then I remembered my talk with the Priest about God's will. It was His will that I felt so terrified in the face of the hunters. Maybe He knew something that I didn't.

This made me feel so good that I almost whistled as I continued walking. I say almost because even if it was God's will that I felt so good that I almost whistled — I knew I could stop myself to avoid scaring off the unicorn. I had learned from the priest that this is called "free will." We all have it — the ability to direct our own actions. The Priest was telling me that Saint Augustine wrote that sometimes free will is influenced by pre-destination. He explained to me that Saint Augustine meant that sometimes God wills or pre-determines that some people will take bad actions and that eventually their evil deeds will have positive outcomes. First, I became skeptical, then bored. Then I started daydreaming. Who could blame me? But now as I reflect on this information, it makes me bristle. Who is to say that Saint Augustine wasn't, at times, delusional? Why wasn't he held up to scrutiny?

I suspected that I wasn't the only one not to believe that God pre-destines evil. In my mind, God represents goodness just as the unicorn does. But it is human nature to project your worst traits onto someone else. It is easy enough to sow discord. Jealously begets jealousy. Anger instills hatred and so forth. But it is also possible to step away from a destructive emotion.

I took a deep breath and walked on. I stepped lightly as if the soles of my feet could sense a life of goodness nearby. I thought that would help me find my beloved unicorn.

Instead, I heard female voices speaking in a fervent hush.

I stopped behind the medlar bush, bent over and saw the bottoms of what must have been two nun's habits brushing each other. Then the bottom of one habit lifted, revealing black wrinkled shoes standing on tip toe. I heard a sound that I had heard before. It was deafening in its silence and roaring in ecstasy. It was the sound of two nuns kissing.

After a long moment, the bottom of the white habit lowered over the black shoes.

There was silence.

"I've been thinking about Sister Beatrice." The one with the deeper voice broke the silence.

I remembered that she was the shorter one and must have been the one who had to stand on her tiptoes.

"Ohh?" said the taller one with the higher voice. She sounded guarded.

"She left so abruptly after the carpenter was here. I hope she is safe with him outside the abbey — if that is indeed where she went," said the one with the deeper voice.

"Oh, Isabella," said the one with the higher voice. "Everyone knows they ran off together, plus the carpenter never returned. I can't help but wonder... we have such little time together ... why are you wasting it by talking about Sister Beatrice?"

"I'm not wasting time by talking about Sister Beatrice," snapped Isabella. It was uncharacteristic of her to be so cross.

I was looking forward to hearing what she said next.

"But if Sister Beatrice did run away with him then it was wrong," continued Isabella. "Mother Superior said so. I distinctly remember her saying that it was wrong — no, "evil" is the word she used — for our Sister Beatrice to put her love for a mere man above her love for God. So how are we different?"

"We are not that different," admitted Heloise. "But we didn't run away. We could never run away together. We could never be accepted in society if we were honest about our love for each other – or if we were found out. We'd be… So maybe it is —"

"worse in our case?" replied Isabella. "I feared the same thing. What we are doing is worse in the eyes of Mother Superior and —"

"in the eyes of God," whispered Heloise in a trembling voice. "You have convinced me."

"We must part," said Isabella quietly. Then distractedly, she said, "I haven't seen Kitty in a while. I'm worried about her."

"Oh. Don't worry about Kitty. I just saw her earlier. She was stalking something," replied Heloise.

She sounded so exasperated that I wondered if she were lying. But she seemed sincere also.

"You seem concerned about Kitty also," observed Isabelle.

"Of course, I am concerned about her. How could I not love a creature that you love so much," replied Heloise.

Isabelle was quiet.

"I agree that we shouldn't see each other, though I wish it wasn't so," continued Heloise softly. "But first make love to me. Let's make love one last time."

I heard a rusting on the other side of the medlar bush. I saw that the bottoms of two white habits as the nuns lay down side by side. I saw the muddy soles of two pairs of black shoes. Then I saw a female hand reach over to pull up one of the habits. I didn't want the women to see me, so I stood and backed away. As I did, I heard a low, guttural sobbing.

I could never believe that God had pre-destined such suffering.

Chapter Twenty-Three

"Love is central to Christianity," said the Priest. "Only when you understand love will you understand Christianity. We hear about love from birth. But most of what we hear about is romantic love."

I nodded. I had never experienced romantic love, but I had heard about it in story after story.

"My mother used to tell me the story of King Arthur and Queen Guinevere. She told me that the Queen also fell in love with her husband's favorite knight, Sir Lancelot, because she was Welsh – and Welsh women were known to be romantically free."

"Hmmm..." responded the Priest. "That may be true, but in the version that I heard the love between Sir Lancelot and Queen Guinevere's remained chaste even after King Arthur's death. Sir Lancelot loved King Arthur too much to betray him."

"See," I responded eagerly. "Two men can love each other, after all."

After I spoke, I sucked in my breath. I was embarrassed that I had spoken without thinking, but I only wanted my teacher to be happy.

I was going to say something, but he spoke first.

"No doubt you are right. That take on it would add another layer to the story," chuckled the priest. But then he sat straighter in his chair — behind his cluttered desk — and turned serious. "But I would be derelict in my duty as your teacher if I didn't mention that the Bible forbids love between two men. It is a sin and it is forbidden." He spoke resolutely as if things like this never happened — as if things like this never happened to men like him. He knew and I knew. And he knew that I knew.

I looked at him blankly.

He met my gaze and continued:

"The thing to remember — if indeed the tale is true and even if it is not — is that this is a cautionary tale. Even in fairy tales, romantic love can go awry."

"Do you mean that it is wrong for a woman to love two men?" I asked innocently.

The priest nodded, commenting, "Of course."

"But my mother said that the Welsh tradition of women being romantically free was important. It reminds women that they cannot be imprisoned forever."

The priest didn't deign to answer. He simply rolled his eyes.

I sensed the priest was hostile to women. I wondered if this was at all connected to his hatred of himself. If he believed what he said about men loving men, he must be full of hatred for his own desires.

But the priest had been so happy lately — more than once I heard him humming at a low register — that I wondered what was causing his happiness. His was usually sad. A glowing countenance replaced his recently drawn face.

I always arrived at his office shortly before he did now. His footsteps behind me signaled his arrival and recently his footsteps were lighter — as if he had suddenly taken up dancing.

One time, I had stopped unexpectedly in his office after class to ask him a question, and Thomas was standing next to his desk. Thomas departed abruptly as if he was ashamed of whatever it was that they were doing.

"The point I was going to make is that romantic love is far from the most important type of love," said the Priest with his usual authority that now was somewhat buoyant. "Christians believe that pure love — the kind of love that is selfless and creates goodness — is the way that God loves us. This is why the saying, 'love you neighbor' is so important. There are numerous references to this in the Bible. But the most important is from the Gospel According to Mark in which he says, 'Love your neighbor as yourself.' There is no commandment greater than these.

"This kind of love is called 'agape,'" continued the priest. "Agape is the highest form of pure, selfless love. It is the kind of love that God has for us — and the kind of love that we strive to have for our fellow man."

"I recognize the word," I replied. "It's Ancient Greek, from the time of Homer."

The Priest narrowed his eyes.

"I see someone's been going to the library again. But learning Greek isn't even on the syllabus for the monks."

"No sir," I responded, lowering my eyes. "I just happened to see the word and remember it and its origins."

I didn't want the Priest to think that I had ambitions of being higher than my station. He seemed to have forgotten that he had observed this about me before.

"That's good," replied the Priest. He appeared to soften but added: "knowing the origins of the word is not the same as understanding the meaning."

I nodded. He was right. No words were needed.

"According to Saint Augustine, it is necessary for us to be able to know the difference between agape — selfless well-intentioned love — and Eros which includes lust and is therefore never selfless. Saint Augustine wrote that the only one we can truly love is God because loving another human incites suspicion, jealousy, anger and fear."

"But that doesn't make sense," I blurted. "How can you love your neighbor if you are afraid of arousing such emotions as jealousy?"

"Loving God is the ideal," said the priest. "What Saint Augustine meant is that we should love our neighbor as if he were God. We should be that kind and patient."

I nodded.

"Therefore, we should love ourselves as if we were God." I said quietly.

"I've never heard it said like that, but yes. But be careful who you tell," he warned. "A statement like that could be interpreted as blasphemy."

I was silent. I certainly didn't want anything I said to be misconstrued.

I nodded.

I was starting to understand. I thought about my favorite quote from the Bible about love. I loved the passage so much that I had committed it to memory and I now recited it to myself silently: *"Love is patient, love is kind. It does not envy, it does not boast, it is not proud."*

But what I said to the Priest was quite different. I don't know why I said it. But it must have been true because my thoughts burst forth from my mouth:

"What about heretics then? Aren't they our neighbors? Shouldn't we love them as much as we love ourselves?"

The Priest raised one eyebrow and narrowed his lips. The look he conveyed was one of skepticism.

"I can see where the naïve person might say this," he stated. "The answer is 'yes.' Heretics are our neighbors. Like a parent — or God the Father — we want the best for them. We want the best for the rest of society also. People influence each other. We don't want the practice of heresy to spread. So, we punish heretics. Then we pray for them."

"And sometimes the Church admits it was wrong," I replied.

"Wrong?" The Priest looked bewildered for a moment.

"Yes, wrong," I stated. "As in the case of The Maid of Orleans."

"Aahh, yes, Joan of Arc. That was one case in which the Church decided to rectify its actions. But remember the Bishop that condemned her was pro-English — even though he lived in the Kingdom of France. If he had lived in our century rather than in 1431 and if he moved away, he might have become a Bishop with the new Church of England. The Church was rectifying the mistake of a traitor when the Pope revisited the trial in 1456, twenty-five years after she was burned to death for heresy. He declared that she was innocent."

"Yes, the people always loved her. My mother and her sisters revered her," I replied reverently.

"Yes," said the Priest solemnly. "She was a real heroine."

I noticed a complete reverence on his part about The Maid. And for the first time, it seemed, he hadn't rolled his eyes when I mentioned my mother.

"Of course, she among women is the exception," he added.

I thought differently. My mother had taught me that women were smart and sensitive. My father, by loving her so much and respecting what she said, had provided me with the example of true, selfless love. But I knew I had to be wary of telling the Priest that I did not agree with him. Instead, I sought to change the topic.

"But back to agape, the kind of love that is selfless and leads to goodness — I realize now that I do understand what you mean," I said.

"I have experienced loving selflessly," I said.

I was thinking of my beloved unicorn. But I had slipped in my love. At first it was selfless — a kind of rapturous awe when I saw her radiance. But then I became possessive and jealous. I wanted her for myself. Maybe it was when I sent the impersonator of the knight in the other direction in his search for the "Holy Grail." But I knew that wasn't when I first felt possessive. I could trace this back to the time when I was watching her in the clearing, and I had become aroused.

When I was feeling this way, I knew that it was wrong. Even when I was a lad in the village and I heard about the older boys snickering about the sheep, I knew that what they were alluding to was wrong. A human and an animal having sexual relations was a sin. It always hurt the animal. How could it be consensual when the animal couldn't speak — at least in the same language as humans? I believed that animals could speak — at least through their actions. That's why they ran away from us. That's why my beloved unicorn wanted nothing to do with humans. We couldn't be trusted.

I had betrayed her by seeking power through the Priest and the Bishop. But now I saw the error of my ways and vowed to love her selflessly, in the agape style of love. That's why I wanted to warn her that she was in danger. I would be honest and tell her everything. That way we could start over. Maybe my beloved unicorn could finally trust me.

I thought of her constantly in a way that was like a prayer. The other day when I was in the library, I learned how to spell "unicorn" in Greek. I felt strongly that if I could unlock her name in this ancient language, I would be closer to finding her we could converse in a common tongue. It was better than finding buried treasure when I found out how to spell her name in Ancient Greek. *Monokeros.*

I remembered tracing my finger over the long lines of the beginning "m" (which stood for *Mu*) and then the circle of the *omicron* that followed, the "v" that was pronounced "n," followed by the second *omicron* (this one with an accent) and then the "k" (standing for *kappa*) and the curves of the "e" (*epsilon*) followed by the "p" that was pronounced "r" followed by the wide curves of the lower-case *omega* and ending in the curves of the *sigma*. I then learned the Ancient Greek spelling of "unicorn" was the product of two words — the first part *mono* meant "alone" and the second part, *keros*, meant "horn." This made sense to me because the unicorn is usually alone and, of course, she has a horn.

Then I remembered that I was meeting with the Priest and looked up.

The Priest was talking in his authoritative tone about the Ten Commandments and how the first five were about selfless love for God.

I found myself becoming skeptical about what he was saying.

The first commandment, which the Priest quoted was: "'I am the Lord thy God, thou shall not have any gods before me.'"

It sounded to me like God was being self-serving when he said that. What if someone needed another god — or God-forbid — a goddess?

I knew enough not to say anything to the Priest, but I must have unconsciously raised an eyebrow in skepticism.

"You would be wise to especially heed the second commandment," said the Priest. "'You shall not make for yourself an idol in the form of anything.'"

The Priest sounded like he was onto me. If he was thinking that the unicorn was beholden to me — above God, above His son — he was right.

But the unicorn wasn't an idol to me. She was my salvation.

Chapter Twenty-Four

I walked along the forest's edge toward the castle where I sensed I would find a maiden who would help me. I stopped and sniffed the air. A sweet virginal female scent wafted in my direction. I was elated! Suddenly everything became more vibrant. The sky was so clear that it was chimerical. I could spend all day staring into it seeing mythical creatures. But I had to keep going. I had to find my maiden who was near! The hills in front of me were closer but still in the distance. The morning mist dissipated.

My ears bent forward. I heard the distant crowing of a cock. I had heard this call before and knew that it was the sign that a new day was starting. Soon people would be walking to the fields to check on their crops. Then wooden carts pulled by horses and sometime peasants would bump up and down on the nearby grassy and muddy ruts.

I knew I would have to be careful, but I felt free. I picked up my hooves as if I were running and bent my knees higher in the air. I was on the scent of a maiden who was going to rescue me. I had eluded the hunters by jumping over the abbey wall.

Happiness is fleeting.

I was pulled back to reality by a rumbling in my stomach. I was hungry. I had been up earlier than usual this morning. I

wanted to find some berries before the birds did. I had been innocently looking for berries when the hunters and the hounds
had ambushed me. I still felt bad about spearing the hound
with my horn and kicking the hunter behind me. I recall that
I could feel the crinkly softness of his cloak on my legs. I still
was appalled at myself about taking part in the violence. But
really what could I have done? The hunters gave me no choice.

I had put out a great deal of energy, and now I was rav-
enous. I was also thinking dreamily of the maiden I would
meet. Maybe this is why I neglected to go into the forest to
eat. It would've been easy enough. There is always thick loamy
vegetation in there that is good to eat. But I didn't want to
run the risk of eating a poisonous mushroom and falling ill.
With every action there is a risk. There is no avoiding this. I
walked on in search of something good to eat. It was breakfast
time and I wanted some fruit — something sweet and juicy.
I thought about pomegranates — maybe some juicy and fermented ones had fallen on the ground. Their juice would give
me the giddy feeling of being free that I had just experienced
on my own. But my belly growled again and that fast I lost
interest. I trudged along looking for something to cease my
hunger pains. I re-thought my quest for fermented pomegranates. They made me giddy — perhaps too giddy. I still had to
keep my wits about me. There would be no rolling on my back
in the field. Besides I didn't want to reek like a tavern, when I
met the special maiden who would come to my rescue.

I followed a trail of blue cornflowers growing at my feet.
Each one looked like a miniature cobalt blue sun with an in-
digo center. I followed the trail until it vanished and then I
looked up and saw a tree standing apart from the forest on my
left. With its wide arc of branches that tapered down from the
horizontal half-moon of its crown, it looked like a regal tree

that was not part of anything larger — not like the trees that grew in the forest. Mighty as the trees were — and they were majestic — they were part of the deep, dark forest. This tree looked as if it stood alone. Even its silvery bark reflected sunlight. The rest of the tree, lush with green leaves, looked perfect. I imagined that it expected the sunlight that shone down on it. Rays of sun shone between the leaves. There was something incandescent about this tree. I was drawn to it like a moth to a light. Then I saw why. I saw the red flecks first — between the green leaves. Then, I saw shiny roundness. Before I knew it, my mouth had finally found breakfast. Hunger sprang forth as I savored the tiny fruits. It felt like I was eating small orbs of sun. I had to stop and spit out the pits and this necessary pause gave me time to think. If I ate too many of the bitterly sweet cherries, I might get a stomach ache. Besides, some other hungry creatures might come along, and I should leave some for them.

I had my fill, being sure to leave plenty for the next hungry creature or creatures who came along, and I ambled forward toward the castle. Looking down at my feet, I noticed that the grass was longer. Then I found myself in a patch of lady's mantle. The wetness of the morning dew was still beaded into the center of its broad and fluted heart shaped leaves. Its tiny yellow flowers were so fragrant that I seemed to fall into a trance and started imaging what I would like to happen.

I wished the warrior princess would valiantly leap to my defense. But even in the sweet idyll of a trance that felt more delightful than rolling on my back after I had eaten fermented pomegranates, I was aware that going back to the clearing – where the warrior princess used to joust with her handmaidens and where a pen now awaits me – would be to walk into a trap. Surely if the warrior princess was acting from her own volition, she would valiantly defend me. But most likely she was influenced by her father the King. He probably had his guards build the wooden pen in the clearing. Maybe he remembered his daughter, the warrior princess, as a little girl. Perhaps she had told him about a passing fancy when she wanted to keep a unicorn as a pet. Lots of little girls loved unicorns. A wish like this — even if she grew out of it — wouldn't be surprising. But it was more likely that the King had heard of the previous King of this same land who had desired a unicorn very badly but was never able to find one. The wise old unicorn I met once told me the story. Not so long ago, this King wanted to possess a unicorn so badly that he ordered the forest people to bring him one. But the forest people hated authority and considered themselves to be the masters of their own fate — not some silly king. Chances are that they sent word to him that they hunted far and wide for a unicorn but couldn't find one. Chances were that they weren't telling the truth. The man or woman who told the messenger this might have snickered inwardly or perhaps outwardly. I felt a kinship with the wild people of the forest because they didn't give a fig about what other people thought. In any event, as the wise old unicorn told me, the King of yesteryear never did get his unicorn. And this new King wanted to fulfill this kingly destiny to reap glory upon himself. But he may have told his daughter that he wanted to capture one because she wanted one as a pet when she was a little girl. Chances are that she would've forgot what she wanted when she was a child and wouldn't oppose her dear father because she thought this sweet. Perhaps he told himself that this was true — even though he probably just wanted glory.

Just then I was jolted out of my trance by an intense itching on my back that felt like some sort of insect was trying to take a bite out of my flesh. I swatted my back with my tail and reminded myself that I needed to get moving so that I could find my special maiden. Surely this maiden would look into my eyes and see that we were soul mates. Then she would want to rescue me.

Just then I heard a full-throated bird song and looked up to see a goldfinch perched on a limb of a tall slender ash tree. I was familiar with the ash because it was one of the few trees that drew lightning to it during a storm. For this reason, I stayed away from it in a thunderstorm. The finch seems to be calling my name in the sounds of an ancient language – *monokeros, monokeros.*

I remember now that the old unicorn told me that many people keep goldfinches as pets. He told me that the finches, though, would rather be free just as most animals would rather be free. I wondered if this finch was one who has escaped a human's home that she used to live in — or whether the humans were kind and let her fly freely during the day.

I had a feeling that the finch was leading me in the right direction. Maybe the maiden would be able to say my name in the ancient language.

Chapter Twenty-Five

My instincts were right!

The finch flitted from ash to elm to oak to holly and finally landed on a low medlar. Daisies scented my path and I walked by primroses with faded yellow petals and golden centers.

I entered another patch of lady's mantle. In the medlar, the finch was chirping my name: *"monokeros, monokeros."*

An intoxicatingly sweet scent wafted in my direction. It felt like the scent was pulling me into another dimension. Then I saw a maiden singing sweetly. She was singing my name in the syllables of an ancient language: *"monokeros, monokeros, monokeros."*

Even though I was entranced by this magical pull, my first instinct was to bolt back into the woods. While I was admiring the daisies and the primroses, I had walked past the end of the forest and stopped in a glade. It was filled with sunlight and a modest but well-built house with an open window upstairs. This must be where the finch flew from.

On the other side of the glade another forest continued — or maybe it was the same forest, but with a clearing. Beyond the woods and to the left, the castle and the low sloping hills were in the background. It occurred to me that all the land was once a forest and that humans had carved villages and the abbeys and even this modest house out of the forest. The land was all moss and trees and shade with rays of light shining through, and there I was standing in the center of the world.

I was just about to follow my instincts and bolt back into the forest, when I turned for one last look at the maiden who was still singing my name sweetly.

We locked eyes. I was still going to turn and run back to the woods. It was in my nature to be skittish around humans – and I was still shy around humans even though I had searched for this one. She was still singing sweetly in the syllables of my name. Then she slowly reached out. Gracefully, she beckoned.

I inhaled her sweet virginal scent and uttered a song that felt familiar, although I did not know where the words came from:

"I am the bride and the bridegroom,
and it is my husband who begot me.
I am the mother of my father
and the sister of my husband
and he is my offspring...
I am the ruler of my offspring.

...

"I am the staff of his power in his youth,
and he is the rod of my old age.
And whatever he wills happens to me."

I do not know if I was singing aloud or if the words stayed in my mind. But I do know that I was in the thrall of the maiden. She was beckoning to me and I was slowly approaching. My legs — all four of them — seemed to be moving according to her will, not my own. She said my name softly as she slowly beckoned with her finger.

Soon my head was in her lap. She was wearing a long red crimson dress with a thin golden chain cinching the waist.

I pushed my nose into the fabric of her dress. It felt as soft as the petals of the red rose that climbed the low fence behind us. Her lap was soft and warm, so comfortable that I felt that I could stay there forever. We were one in our vulnerabilities, our innocence and our imagination — because imagination demands innocence and vulnerability. Surely the maiden would sense that she had more in common with me than with anyone — particularly the lord of the house if there was one.

Then I felt a slight shift as if the maiden had stopped stroking me and lifted her arm to signal someone.

The lord of the house! Of course, there must be one. What was I thinking? Just then I smelled the presence of a hunter and his hounds. The maiden stood up. The hound jumped on my back and bit me. I felt warm blood tricking down my sides.

It was a trap!

The maiden was not as pure as she had pretended to be.

I had been betrayed. The ground seemed to open under me, and it would've swallowed me. But at that same moment I felt the hound let go of my back and even though I felt a second hound nipping at my heels, I knew that this was my chance to bolt.

As I did, I saw a flash of a hunter stepping out from behind the holly tree that stood with the oak and the apple tree in a small grove next to the garden. He was about to blow into his horn — to signal the other hunters. I also saw the maiden waving to the hunter. I almost couldn't believe that she had betrayed me. But equally strong was the thought, *how could I have been so gullible?* Of course, she had betrayed me. I was a fool to think we had so much in common. Most likely she was instructed by the lord of the manor to work with the hunters because they would reward her amply. She probably never thought about me — thinking instead of her own gain. She probably had laughed with the lord of the manor and the hunters when she was plotting with them to kill me. The lord of the manor was probably her father, since she still smelled so sweet and virginal.

But the hunters probably sensed that she would not be a virgin for long as she laughed with them. Perhaps the hunters had been intoxicated by her sweetness just like I had. Maybe they were already laying designs on her. Her innocence was like the new moon, invisible to the naked eye, but in silhouette, an eclipse in front of the sun. She seemed like a blank slate in her innocence. But she already had her own motives.

I didn't know where I was going, but I knew I had to flee from the maiden and her friends the hunters. I had to flee from this place.

As I ran, the tree, the bushes the flowers became a green and yellow blur that I sped by. I could feel tufts of grass thrust by my hooves as they bit into the ground in a desperate gallop.

Betrayal became a bitter taste in my mouth.

Chapter Twenty-Six

I held a leaf in my hand and examined it. It was shiny and green and looked like fingers in a mitten, so it must have been from an oak tree. I counted seven clusters. There was a vein running vertically down the leaf. Offshoots of the vein travelled into the clusters that looked like fat green fingers. The exception was the top lobe in the shape of three short, webbed fingers. The vines that went into it looked like the three lines of the Greek *Psi*.

I had the morning off. I had eaten the chunk of stale bread that was my usual breakfast and went to morning mass. Now I strolled through the abbey. I walked as near the stone wall as I could, careful of vines and sticker bushes. I wanted to avoid other humans — which wasn't hard in the abbey since I rarely saw anyone else. I still hadn't found my beloved unicorn so that I could warn her that the hunters were after her — and that she should go far, far away. But I figured if she was in the abbey, she would be here near the stone wall and far away from the structures.

I wondered where she was.

I stepped slowly, softly. I took another step. A branch snapped under my foot. I winced. That would never do. If my beloved unicorn heard that she would assume there was a human nearby — big enough to snap a branch under foot — and hide. It seemed like I would never find her. I decided to pray. But I had prayed to the One God before several times and it hadn't worked. Who would I pray to? Who would help me?

Immediately, the Goddess Bastet leapt to mind. Bastet was an Egyptian Goddess – half woman and half cat. I knew about her because when I was a boy, my mother would tell me the stories that her father had told her. He had loved Greek mythology and found out that the Goddess Artemis, the goddess of the hunt, was related to the earlier Goddess Bastet who came from the earlier fierce lioness Goddess Bast, the warrior goddess of the sun.

The followers of Bastet ruled ancient Egypt for a time in the land where cats were sacred. I remember that my mother's emerald green eyes gleamed as if she was a cat herself when she told me about the Goddess Bastet who kept away disease and was the protector of pregnant women. The stories she told me about the fierce, soft, cat Goddess Bastet were so vivid that she made me want a cat for my very own pet.

My mother cautioned me, however, not to mention cats to anyone but her. People with cats were looked on with suspicion, she warned me. The Church looked down on cats as wily creatures associated with Satan. Again, my mother told me that it was very important never to anger the Church.

Surely, the Goddess Bastet would help me find my beloved unicorn. She of all the gods and goddesses would understand why I had to find my beloved unicorn to save her.

I closed my eyes tightly until I saw a slim woman, standing tall with very good posture, with the head of a cat. I knew it was Goddess Bastet, just as my mother had described her.

Silently, I began to pray:

O Holy Goddess,

You of all the holy ones have the power to lead me to my sacred creature, the unicorn. She is as important to the world as she is to me. Yet the hunters are after her. It is my fault. I led them to her out of the sin of Pride. I regret that I did this and am deeply sorry. I have offended all creatures in doing so. If you can help me find her, I will be gratefully indebted to you forever. I will make offerings in your name. I will forever swear off eating the meat of any animal. I know that you are descended from a fierce lioness who must have eaten her share of prey. I know that it is not bad to eat flesh. But if I do not eat flesh, there will be more for the animals.

I stopped praying then and edited my thoughts and corrected my prayer.

For the other animals, I thought (for is it not true that we are all animals?) and then continued praying. *For I am an animal like you — half man and half unicorn. At least in my heart, I am half beast.*

Then I stopped praying again and thought, *not beast, I mean unicorn as in I am half unicorn.*

I continued praying:

I can see her because I am like her. I am pure at heart. Or at least I was. But then I made a very bad mistake. Everyone makes mistakes, but this one was very bad. I won't tell you what I did, because you will think less of me. I am begging you for forgiveness. Didn't you ever kill a mouse out of instinct, blindly, and then realize what you did and then have remorse. What I did was instinctual, too. I wanted power. I wanted to get ahead. I saw the other monks and aspiring priests scheming to get ahead. But I didn't want to get ahead by doing the things that they were doing — even if I could have. By the time I realized what I had done, I abhorred my own behavior. I truly repent.

Amen.

I had also learned from my mother that the Greeks who had lived in ancient Egypt had changed the Goddess Bastet into a goddess of the moon. I can still hear my mother saying, "I guess they felt they had to do something different." Then she hid her snicker behind her hand.

The cat goddess was known as *Ailuros* in Greek mythology. I sounded out the Greek letters in my mind starting with *alpha, iota, lambda, omicron, upsilon, rho, omicron,* and ending with *sigma. Ailuros.*

I thought about praying to the Greek cat goddess, but then reconsidered. If the Greek cat goddess was just the Greek version of the Egyptian Goddess Bastet, then there might be a problem. I didn't want to anger the Egyptian Goddess Bastet. After all, she was part human and she may be angry that the Greeks had occupied her land for a time and that they even claimed that their Goddess Artemis was related to the earlier Goddess Bastet who was a fierce warrior.

If only there was a goddess of the unicorn. I thought for a moment and decided that would be an oxymoron because the unicorn was a goddess. I shrugged and asked myself, why not? There could be a unicorn goddess and if there wasn't one, what harm was there in making one up?

I recited her name in the Ancient Greek — *monokeros* — as if it were an incantation.

Monokeros, monokeros, monokeros.

I repeated my ancient chant and closed my eyes. Then I opened them and looked around. Nothing.

I found myself saying *pss...tt—* which my mother had told me was an ancient Egyptian word for the Goddess Bastet.

I said it again, "*pss...tt.*"

Just then a gray striped cat ran out from under a nearby medlar bush. I was so shocked that I stood still as a statue as she wrapped her shiny furry body around my legs at the bottom of my brown robe. Then I did what came naturally. I reached down and petted her. She was as magical as I had imagined: silky, furry and warm. A contented sound, like the rough breathing from the back of the throat that I was learning about in the ancient Greek, met my ears. She seemed happy to see me.

Was she related to the Goddess Bastet? I wondered. *Was she the goddess herself?*

To me it was all spirit.

But I knew enough to be quiet about it since I didn't want to be called a pagan or a heretic. Maybe this is what the Priest had meant when he said to me that the monks are taught enough to know when they should be silent. It was a warm day, but I shivered for a moment as I pondered the fate of heretics.

Time was slipping through my fingertips. Seven weeks had passed since the feast day of Pentecost. Pentecost celebrated the day that the Holy Ghost descended to the apostles, often in the form of a dove through the "holy ghost" hole that was built into the ceiling of many cathedrals. Even our little church in the abbey had a "holy ghost" hole over the sanctuary. I was disappointed when I overheard that a workman had been hired to release the dove through the ceiling. In other words, the dove did not fly into the church of its own accord. What bird would? They never come inside unless it is by mistake. And then they are in a panic to get back outside again. I was disappointed because I felt it was manipulative and an untruth. But I was starting to understand the Holy Ghost. That feeling of being infused with light and awe was how I felt when I saw my beloved unicorn.

I felt bad about the workman having to go on the church roof on the feast day of the Pentecost. But truth be told, I felt far worse for the dove. When I was a boy, my mother had told me that the dove was always associated with goddesses. I remember her mentioning Aphrodite, Venus and Isis. My mother told me that the dove was used in Christianity to attract followers who must at some level remember the old ways. I have no doubt that this is true. But a dove is also a dove — and not just a symbol. It is a living creature. The poor thing — shoved down a hole and forced to go inside the church. And if creatures have souls which I believe they do — why not? They are distinct like us and each one has its own personality — the dove would know that it was being forced to participate in a lie.

I looked around again. I was standing in beauty — green trees stretched up to the bell of an azure sky. But there was no unicorn in sight. And the cat — if I had really seen her and had not imagined the whole thing — was long gone. *Would I find my beloved unicorn in time?*

Who else could I pray to?

Who could help me?

I thought about praying to Saint Anthony, the patron saint of lost things. He was also known as the "Professor of Miracles" and the "Hammer of Heretics." He was born in Lisbon in 1195 and lived to 1231. One of the most popular Saints, he was a Portuguese Catholic Priest and became known for his moving sermons and his love for the poor.

Saint Anthony is prayed to for help finding lost things because once he had a book of psalms that was special to him because it contained his notes used in teaching. The book was stolen by a novice who had decided to leave the order. When he observed that it was gone, Saint Anthony prayed for its return. God must have heard his prayers. The thief not only returned the book of palms but also decided to rejoin the order.

The book became one of Saint Anthony's attributes. He was also associated with the white lily stalk because it represented purity.

I am also pure of heart. I will pray to him.

I closed my eyes and concentrated with all my might:

> *Dear Saint Anthony,*
>
> *You are known as the Saint to pray to for the retrieval of lost things, including souls. I have lost a soul who is dear to me so I hope you will hear my petition. I have lost my beloved unicorn. But first I betrayed her. I was just acting naturally — and unwittingly committed the sin of Pride and ambition. But then I realized the error of my ways, and I am truly sorry. I must find her to warn her that the hunters are after her and that the Bishop told the hunters. And I told the Bishop. I regret that I did so but, with your help, maybe I can catch her in time and save her.*
>
> *Amen*

I had never prayed to a saint before. I felt a little foolish as if I were just praying to someone like me who had been exalted by the Church. But I believed in Saint Anthony and needed his help. Still to me, the ending seemed a little formal. So, I added:

And thank you.

I waited for a moment and then opened my eyes and looked around. Again, nothing. The grounds around me were beautiful in their overgrowth. They heralded summer. Vines stretched toward sun. But there was no unicorn and no sign that I should follow a certain direction to find her. I felt foolish. I had prayed to a saint known as the "Hammer of Heretics" about my unicorn. Most likely Saint Anthony would think me a heretic for being so concerned with her.

Even if he heard my prayers, he would dismiss me as a heretic. Thank god, he was only a saint and couldn't smote me down.

I thought about praying to God the Father. But I had prayed to him about the unicorn before and He didn't give me any response.

Well, He might have more important things to think about, I thought. Clearly, I was desperate.

Plus, he might be angered by the fact that I had prayed to the cat goddess, a mere saint, and called on an imaginary unicorn goddess, before I thought of Him again.

I looked down at my feet. A shortish fern stood out from the undergrowth and curled in the high grass. I knelt over and plucked it from the ground. Starting at the bottom, the fronds that should have been longer — were eaten almost to the main stem in the middle. I say almost, because there was the nub of the frond on each side of the stem. I turned the fern over and admired the tiny golden spores on the light green leaves. Then I counted the nubs of the leaves that were missing. The ragged edges looked like a small creature — maybe a wood mouse — had eaten the fronds. There were exactly seven nubs of eaten off leaves on each side of the stem.

I thought about the number seven. I had learned from my mother that it was a sacred number. She had learned from her father that the seven stars of the Pleiades, the seven sisters, were the daughters of the Titan named Atlas and the nymph known as Pleiades.

I still remember my mother holding my hand in the immense darkness as we gazed up at the stars and identified the ones that shone more brightly. These, I came to learn, were the planets.

There were seven spheres that we looked for. Although their positions seemed to change in the night sky, we could identify them. My mother told me that ancient civilizations worshipped the sun and the stars and the planets.

Gazing up at the stars when I was a boy made me wonder. And now, holding the fern in my hand, I wondered again:

Could the sacred number seven help me find my beloved Unicorn?

Chapter Twenty-Seven

I was fleeing from the maiden and her friend the wicked hunter with his hounds.

It's almost impossible to ambush someone with hounds. They are always yelping and making smells, so they are usually easy to detect. I suppose the hunter brought the hounds in hope that they would attack me. Even though I was galloping, I could feel the trickle of blood running down from the gash on my back. As fast as I ran, I could not leave the pain behind.

I still felt betrayed by the maiden, but I tried not to feel too betrayed. I liked to lay my head in the maidens' laps and at times I daydreamed that they loved me. But I suppose they loved themselves more. That is, they had their own interests at heart. They thought the men — including the wicked hunters — were going to rescue them. I imagine some of the men were kind and did put them up in big castles where they were so cold, they wore furs on top of their fancy gowns. Thinking of people wearing furs made me shudder. The wise old unicorn had told me that some humans did this and that you could never trust a person who wore a fur for decoration — even for warmth. Before you know it, they would be wearing your hide. Or in the case of the wise old unicorn and myself, the humans would be displaying parts of our severed horns as status symbols on their grand dining tables. These were just the nobles, of course. I had observed that there were far more people who lived in small homes in the woods or in tents in the cemeteries. And there were the men who lived on one side of the abbey and the silent women at the far end. Then there were the wild people in the woods. The fact that I liked them so much was why let some of the wild women ride me. My back was bare of a saddle, and they were naked also. In this way they let me know that we were related.

But the wise old unicorn also told me that most men were still barbarians. They might pretend they were chivalrous, but they were often violent to their wives in private — and in those drafty old castles they could do anything without being detected. The maiden who betrayed me probably was like many maidens who thought the men — even the wicked hunters — would rescue them and take care of them. Only some would be lucky.

But it made sense that many of them would be surprised. They would be treated like they had treated me, but worse. They would be betrayed and abused. At least I had only been betrayed. But I guess the hunters intended on abusing me. I admit that I felt better by thinking that I had only been betrayed – but now I see everything more plainly. I didn't wish abuse on the women. My thinking was just logical. I only hoped they would come to their senses. I hoped that given time, they would come to realize that we had more in common than they thought. I did not wish to rescue them or for them to rescue me either. If we couldn't be equals, I wished for them to remember that they had once loved me and that this meant something. I wished them well.

As I galloped away from the maiden and her friend the wicked hunter and his hounds, I did not stop to think of which direction I was going. I had to flee. I knew that much — and for a while the fact of fleeing was enough.

Trees and flowers rushed past me in a green blur that was flecked with white, red, yellow, and pale pink blurring into deep magenta. I could tell from the purple dots below my feet that the ground was studded with violets. But I had no time to stop.

A few long-horn brown cows were grazing in the field to my right that had been cleared from the woods.

"Mo -," said the cow, stopping before the entire sound was uttered.

Out of the corner of my eye, I saw the cow look up in wide-eyed astonishment as I galloped by. I imagined that the cow hadn't seen my kind before and didn't know what to make of me.

I suspected that I had outrun the hunter and his hounds, so I slowed down. The forest I trotted next to looked familiar. A path snaked into the woods. I remembered taking it through the woods and coming out into the clearing where I looked in the window of the little house and saw an image of myself being woven into the tapestry. I remembered seeing the circular pen and the collar around my neck and shuddered. I wasn't going back there again — even though I would be safer in the woods.

I realized that I was headed back in the direction of the abbey.

I knew I wasn't safe in the abbey — even though it still felt like home to me. There were probably hunters there waiting for me. But the hunters could be anywhere.

Was I safe anywhere?

I certainly didn't want to run in the other direction toward the castle — and risk being seen by the King. I still had hopes that his daughter the warrior princess would save me.

I knew, however, that my hopes were not rational. Although in my heart I hoped she had run away and was leading the men in battle or a crusade of some sort. If this were true, her absence would be the reason that she wasn't coming to my rescue.

I knew that soon I would be at the abbey wall. I picked up speed and began to gallop as fast as the wind. I could feel my heels digging into the earth. I imagined that the wind propelled brown clumps of dirt behind me. Then I thought of nothing but my strength, tensed my muscles and jumped so high that it felt like I was flying as I leapt over the abbey wall.

It felt safe in the abbey. It was quiet and there were no cows staring at me. Most importantly, I didn't see any hunters waiting for me. Maybe they assumed I would run in the opposite direction and were waiting near the castle.

In the quietness of the abbey, the chirping of the birds boomed.

I listened so intently that I could hear the birds talking to each other.

I spotted a smallish speckled bird, that looked like a grouse, sitting on the low branch of a nearby tree and chirping loudly: "I heard there are hunters nearby," said the bird. "But don't worry, apparently they aren't hunting ducks."

At first, I thought that the bird was talking to no one in particular. But then I noticed a slightly smaller sparrow, with black markings under its eyes and beak and darker brown feathers on its back, sitting in the branches of a tree some ways away. No wonder the first bird was chirping so loudly.

"How do you know that the hunters aren't hunting ducks?" asked the sparrow.

"The hunters have javelins that they sometimes use to throw at ducks," the grouse replied. "But tell your duck friends not to worry. I heard from a very knowledge friend — a falcon — that they are just hunting that silly unicorn down there."

I started. First of all, I didn't appreciate being referred to as silly. Who does? And second, the fact that the bird was insulting me to my face meant that he didn't think I could understand his chirps. But I didn't act angry. Instead, I walked over to a daisy, put my head down, sniffed its white petals, and listened.

"Oh, a falcon," said the house sparrow. "Then it must be true."

I snorted into the flower. Why birds looked up to the falcon was beyond me. In the animal world, domesticated animals — such as hounds — were looked at with contempt. But birds seemed to have a different pecking order.

I sniffed the flower again and then looked up just in time to see the sparrow flying away. He must be flying to his duck friends to tell them they were safe. I noticed that the first bird didn't say where the hunters were — inside the abbey or outside the walls —or when he had seen them. That was so like a bird to be imprecise. It was amazing that they could fly around without smashing into things.

Disgusted, I wandered down to the East wall of the abbey — where the silent women lived. For some reason, I felt that I was less likely to find hunters there.

I approached the stone structure where the women lived. I didn't feel like being seen so I hid behind a medlar bush.

"Here, Kitty, Kitty," said a low female voice.

"There you are," replied a higher female voice. "I saw you leave the convent and decided to come after you. You've been avoiding me. I guess you really don't love me anymore."

"Not love you!" exclaimed the lower female voice. "Even though we have parted, I think about you every day."

I bent my head down to smell the pungent musk of a clary plant. This way my horn was down too, which meant the women were less likely to see me.

It was so rare that I heard women's voices in the abbey that I didn't want to startle them.

"In fact, you're all I think about — when I am eating, sleeping, doing my devotions," said the one with the lower voice. "But still, I forced myself to stay away from you, because I thought it was the right thing."

I suspected that these two women were the ones I had spied before. They seemed to be the only women here who had the courage to talk.

"What a relief, Isabella," said the one with the higher voice. "You're all I think about, too. I was sick thinking that you didn't love me anymore."

Her voice trembled, but she sounded excited too — as if she couldn't believe she was finally seeing her beloved.

"Heloise, I could never not love you. I tried to stay away from you but failed. Perhaps I am not worthy of being a nun."

"Nonsense," replied Heloise. "If God wanted us to be apart, it wouldn't be so painful for us."

"That's true, Heloise. You are so wise. I cannot resist you. Come here and kiss me."

There was a long moment of silence that ended with the soft sound of two lips parting. I can sense energies — from gentleness to aggression — and what was going on between these two women was very gentle and loving.

"What's this?"

I heard the tinkling of small metal pieces touching each other.

"That's just a relic that I have been wearing around my neck," replied Isabella. "It's the imprint of a dove, which of course, means that I'm close to Jesus. I've been wearing it for strength, but I still can't resist you."

"The fact that we love each other so much means that we are fated to be together," replied Heloise. "God approves. In fact, he has chosen us for his special love."

Chapter Twenty-Eight

"I was re-reading Aquinas recently and began to see things differently," said my teacher.

"Really?"

I hoped that I didn't sound too eager. But could it be that my interest in Aquinas stirred the Priest to re-read him?

"Augustine takes a hard line on lust and blames the sinner. Aquinas, however, writes that lust is natural. He writes that it is simply 'the craving for pleasurable good' and that this is a natural state."

The Priest was talking as if I wasn't there. In fact, he wasn't even looking at me.

It was two days after my walk — when I had prayed to the Goddess Bastet and to Saint Anthony to help me find my beloved unicorn.

I was happy for the Priest that he had re-read Aquinas and come to a place of self-acceptance. But I was agitated that I still hadn't found my beloved unicorn despite my prayers — or was it because of them? Was it simply fate?

The Priest was studying the wall behind me or maybe he was waiting for someone to walk by the open door behind me — Thomas maybe — who was now the object of the Priest's attention. I had noticed that the Priest had a spring in his step when he came into the office behind me. Could it be that he was planning a future together with Thomas? If they were to live together, they would have to leave the abbey (where after all love was preserved for God). I tried to imagine them living in a little house in a village — any village. It was hard — no impossible — to imagine the townspeople accepting them as a couple. At best, they would certainly run the two men out of town. They would be forced to go to the nearest city where they would have more of a chance. Aquinas might be more liberal in his writings than Augustine, but that still wasn't saying much. I wonder who would be thought of as more of a heretic, if my obsession with my beloved unicorn and the Priest's likely relationship with Thomas came to public notice. We'd probably be in the same line for the pyre.

I didn't say any of this, of course. Despite that the Priest was still not looking at me, I smiled and replied:

"You can't deny your nature. You were created by God after all."

I really did wish my teacher well. I wished him happiness with Thomas, and I hoped no one would find out. But something was nagging at me. *The unicorn. I had to find my beloved unicorn.*

The Priest dropped his gaze and looked at me levelly.

"I think these conversations with you have helped me — even though I *am* the teacher," he said.

I raised my eyebrows and said nothing. I had nothing to say. He was right. He was the teacher and, as such, he had more power in this conversation. That's why I kept my thoughts to myself so often. It is also why I aspired to be a priest. Even if it meant that I was aspiring for something beyond my station, it meant that I would be important, and that people would listen to me. *I would be somebody.*

Monks weren't thought of as important people. That's why I wanted to be a priest. That was the only way that I could be an important person. Monks were known for being silent and praying all day. But we did many other things — like hauling the slop for the pigs and building water wheels. We did backbreaking work — yet we weren't respected for that. The only people who had it worse than us were the nuns. The nuns in the abbey were forbidden to speak at all. The monks could only say what the Priests' wanted to hear. I wondered if being a monk really was better than being a nun who had taken a vow of silence. If I had to betray my beloved unicorn to get ahead, maybe it wasn't worth it.

I nodded.

"You mentioned your mother frequently. I realized that every time you did so, I was dismissive. Then I realized it was because I didn't want to remember my own mother — or the absence of her."

I looked at him wordlessly. How wise he was to realize the cause of his actions.

"I hope you can forgive me."

I nodded again, this time saying sincerely, "I forgive you."

"That's good," he replied crisply. "You know Christianity expects forgiveness. That's why we confess our sins during lent — so we can do our penances and purify ourselves for the year to come." He sounded very formal, almost businesslike.

I nodded. But I was thinking something else. Suddenly the question burst forth out of my mouth:

"But what about when something happens that can't be forgiven?"

I was thinking about myself — about my betrayal of my beloved unicorn. I felt very guilty. Try as I might, I could not forgive myself.

"Forgiveness starts with the self," answered the Priest. That is the first step and then it is necessary to confess the sin out loud. Then the absolution of your sins will help you. After you do penance you will feel better."

I nodded glumly.

"I could tell something was weighing on you since the beginning of our meeting," continued the Priest.

He could? How could he tell what was going on in my mind, when he wasn't even looking at me? Despite being startled by his insight, I thought quickly. I could not tell him that I felt guilty about betraying my beloved unicorn and had had a change of heart. First, he would tell me that betraying my beloved unicorn wasn't a sin and that I shouldn't feel guilty. Then he would tell me she might not even be real. Lastly, he would tell me that this kind of thinking made me a heretic. Heretics weren't forgiven, were they?

Then I thought of something. It was true, so I wasn't making things worse by lying.

"Now that you told me why you dismissed my comments about my mother, I do forgive you. But I am having a hard time forgiving myself, for having had bad feelings toward you whenever you dismissed my mother."

"But it's natural to want to defend your mother, and to feel badly toward anyone who derides her. I would defend my mother except that I never really knew her. She died shortly after I was born — as a result of giving birth to me. It was understandable that I preferred to think that I didn't have a mother, to feeling sad about her absence. But my older sister – who was unusual among women – always told me that my mother was a wonderful woman and that I would have loved her."

He stopped to wipe a tear from his eye.

"I forgive you about thinking badly of me when I made dismissive comments about your mother. I just hope you can forgive me."

I nodded. I really did forgive him even though I still couldn't forgive myself for betraying my beloved unicorn.

"After I began thinking about my mother, I began thinking that I really should give more credit to women. Take the Maid for example."

"The Maid of Orleans? I asked.

The Priest nodded.

"I've been thinking that she really got a bad deal," he said. "She saved France when she was just a girl really. She was born fifty years after the black death took nearly half the population of France. She died less than a century ago. Many of the people who were left after the Black Death died in The Hundred Years War. And then the King she helped crown betrayed her. Who else was going to save France? There weren't that many men left really."

"My mother told me that the Maid heard voices in her head since childhood. And that they were the voices of fairies," I said.

"Fairies?! I never heard such a thing. Fairies were pagan. Joan was a devout Christian and she knew that claiming that the voices in her head were from fairies would have been heresy."

The Priest eyed me with the authority of one who had been there — regardless that her trial was almost a hundred years ago.

"The voices in her head were the voices of the Saints," he stated.

I must have had a look on my face, because almost immediately the Priest softened.

"It is natural for mothers to tell their children tales — including tales of the fairies talking to the Maid of Orleans.

Most women are like children and therefore can be excused for telling such tales," he said.

I said nothing. I wondered if this was one of those moments where forgiveness was expected.

An awkward silence fell between us.

I noticed that the stack of books that had been on the edge of his desk were missing.

"I had been meaning to ask you what those books were on the edge of your desk." I pointed as I spoke.

"Oh, them. They were just books about having faith in numbers. I had been intending to give them away, but I didn't want them traced back to me because the topic is controversial. Finally, I just dropped them into the furnace next to the scullery," said the Priest.

"You burned books!?" I was aghast.

The Priest shrugged. "Usually, I wouldn't. But I recently heard that the Church categorically condemns all books that talk about the belief in mystical relationships between numbers and events."

I sat up straight. I had been wondering if the magical number seven could help me find my beloved unicorn. Here was my chance to learn more.

"Are you sure the furnace was on when you dropped the books in there?" I asked.

"Actually, I'm not sure," answered the Priest. "Why? You're not going to try to retrieve the books, are you?"

I shrugged. "It would be a shame to see good books go to waste. And I've heard such good things about the faith in numbers. Augustine believed in using numbers for divination. The Bible is full of not so secret numbers, starting with the world being made in seven days and seven nights."

"Augustine believed in astrology for a time too," replied the Priest. "That doesn't mean it was right. The Church has changed its position on the faith in numbers. That's enough for me. Besides, numbers are dangerous."

"Numbers are dangerous?" I really didn't understand.

"Numbers are Arabic. They're from Islamic lands. And we can't trust the Saracen. They're known for killing the crusading Christians by brutally by severing their heads.

I had heard this story, too, but it happened a century or so ago — not recently.

I was about to tell the Priest. But then I saw the stern look on his face — the ridges in his tensed forehead, the vein bulging in his neck. I knew this look meant that the Priest was convinced he was right, no matter what anyone else said.

Chapter Twenty-Nine

I was in the East end of the abbey backing away from the embracing female humans with their white habits. I took one last glance. They were embracing next to a tree, and then they slunk down behind a medlar bush.

I had to admit that I still felt superior to them — since I could achieve that state of love all by myself — without the drama and the angst. But I also felt compassion for the women. If they loved each other, they should be allowed to be together. It was obvious they were unhappy at the thought that they had to part. In a way, they were like me. They could only be themselves when they hid. But their solitude included the other while mine just included me. The other major thing that was different between us was that I craved solitude. I suspected that if they were accepted for who they were and could be open about their love for each other, they would be happy.

I was happy to be alive. Maybe it was facing death so often that changed me. I had escaped from the hunters four times, five if you count the first time the hunters, wearing their finery and their plumes to impress each other, gathered in the abbey to look for me. The second time was when I dipped my horn into the stream that flows in front of the fountain. The fountain behind me seemed to offer protection with its sound of water splashing on stone. But when I look at the tapestry, I see a ring of hunters. Their hounds had gathered in a half circle behind the fountain. The hunters and their hounds are in the top half of the tapestry on the wall. This was where I see that my young human "friend" with one eye bigger than the other, wearing a long brown robe and with a horn slung over his shoulder, is pointing me out.

I escaped the hunters again, depicted in another tapestry, when I was jumping over another stream and the javelin-wielding hunters and their hounds surrounded me. Then I escaped the hunters and their hounds again, the time I was forced to defend myself — when I kicked a hunter with my back hooves and with my horn speared a hound until he bled. As I said before, I usually don't like to injure anyone — especially other animals — but what else could I do? Then I leapt over the abbey wall and near the castle found a maiden who tamed me. I laid in her lap only to find that she had signaled the hunters who waited nearby. Somehow the tapestry maker captured this scene too – in another tapestry. Being betrayed by this maiden made me distrust the rest of the maidens — or at least most of them — who put what they think are their own interests above mine. I was going to say that I guess they have their reasons but, really, they are of no concern to me.

I felt safer back in the abbey. I felt this way despite the silly birds — who had the nerve to call *me* silly – who said they overheard that the hunters are looking for me. I knew logically, that I was not safe anywhere. But I felt safer in the abbey than outside of it. I guess it felt like home to me. It was quieter there and the people who lived there were sparse and contemplative. I knew that my "friend" lived there — but like the maidens he seemed to have more an allegiance to the hunters. But he was still the closest thing to a friend that I had. I saw him grow from a lad, with a pure heart, to a young man who still had that pure heart before he seemed suddenly capable of betrayal. Perhaps most humans were once pure at heart and then something happens — maybe something injures them, or they just succumb to the corruptness that surrounds them — and they become capable of betrayal.

It felt like home here because I saw and smelled the familiar plants, including the musky sage with its bluish green wide leaves, the clary with its tall and dark mauve flowers. There were also white lilies, as bright as me, and wild roses as red as blood, and the thorny St. Mary's thistle with its succulent bright purple flower with its milky center. Even though I did not put down my head to taste the plants, I knew I could. In the distance (but not too far away), I saw the pomegranate trees with their tasty reddish blue bruised orbs nestled among the deep green leaves. Behind them, the mighty oak tree leaves seemed to smile at me. The tufts of grass at my feet — and the breezes in the dome of sky above me — seemed to whisper my name.

I could not see the other animals — only the rabbit who nibbled on clary leaves about thirteen feet from me. But I knew that they were there. Somewhere — hiding in this abbey, maybe waiting for me to purify a stream — was my equal, the lion. And he and his regal mate would most likely be joined by the wily red fox, the laughing hyena and the stag who might still be sulking. Even the conformist sparrows — who I could hear in the trees but not see — were here at home with me. And somewhere the serpent slithered. Even though I had to cleanse the streams of her venom so the others could drink — I still respected the serpent. I stood very still and sensed the vibrations of all the animals.

Even the spirit of my old friend the late Great Lion who I saw die was here. I remember now that I had been sitting with him and that I was sobbing softly. I was trying not to show it, because I had heard somewhere that the sound of tears falling has the intensity of the worst rainstorm when someone is dying. But I couldn't help myself. I was extremely sad. I was crying because I loved the lion and could not imagine life without him. How could a great a creature as the lion cease to exist? We were so close that he was like a father to me. But I remember now that I felt the vibration of a kind of rectangular and pure place open in the sky to receive him. I remember now that I felt a huge sense of relief. He had lived his life. He had completed the hard work of staying alive. It was fitting that he died in the abbey — in such a quiet, contemplative place. Even the church was quiet the day he died. The quietness was a kind of forever.

The appearance of the group of hunters and their hounds that appeared later could not take the forever away.

I heard the hush of eternity when the Great Lion died.

I sniffed the air. I did not smell any hounds. My back felt fine — as if the trickle of my blood had dried or even as if the wound had magically disappeared. I felt a warm breeze on my face. It was soft like the hand of the wind — as if a wild woman was murmuring to me.

I was alive.

I was home. I could feel it in the thrum of everything around me. Even the insects seemed to rub their legs together in the cadence of my name. *Monokeros, monokeros.*

Even knowing that I may be hunted down here — compared to being somewhere else where I was fearful that the hunters might find me — made the abbey feel even more like home.

I could meet my end here, like the Great Lion.

I wonder how a place that could be dangerous, could feel like home.

For some, a place that contains the threat of violence can especially feel like home.

For the moment I was safe.

But I knew that moments rarely last.

Chapter Thirty

I was captured because I was entranced by a patch of English daisies. The petals were tinged with pink and there was a yellow center. There was a patch of the flowers near the place in the abbey where the silent women lived.

I was just about to approach the path, when I heard voices.

"Oh, look — a patch of Mary flowers," said a woman.

"Shhhh. We're not allowed to speak," said a lower female voice.

"What does it matter, the Mother Superior is not here," said the first woman.

I quickly hid behind a medlar bush. I suspected that these women were the ones I had left behind a short while ago. They must have finished their loving and were wandering around like me, looking at flowers.

"But we have been gone so long, that she might come looking for us and hear us," replied the one with the lower voice.

"Maybe, the Mother Superior will think that she is delusional and hearing voices. Maybe she will think that she hears the voice of God and that She is female..." The woman with the higher voice paused. "Maybe I shouldn't say that to you. Surely you think me blasphemous."

She was met by silence. Finally, the woman with the lower voice spoke:

"Actually, I think you may be on to something. Maybe God is a woman. How are we to know?"

Now, it was the other woman's turn to be silent.

Then she spoke:

"Yes, you are right, my beloved. How are we to know? Certainly, the church fathers would cover it up if God was a woman. I bet the Mother Superior would cover it up too. If she had the time, I bet she'd wander the abbey too because it is so beautiful and when she found the Mary flower, she would pick its petals slowly, saying 'He loves me, He loves me not.' Or maybe she'd be saying, 'She loves me, She loves me not.'" Then the woman with the higher voice had been speaking. She broke into a titter.

The other one giggled so gruffly that she sounded like she was giggling reluctantly. Then she said, "I never got that impression from her. She's probably so miserable that she never has any kind of attraction. Seriously, though, we should go back before someone comes looking for us."

"Ok," said the first one. "I'll follow you but then wait a while after I enter the convent. We don't want anyone to think we've been together."

I waited a long time behind the medlar bush. Then when the coast was clear, I retraced my steps to the English daisy, lowered my head and inhaled the spicy sweet fragrance of the succulent flower. I discovered that there was a trail of English daisies. Intoxicated by the vapors, I followed the flowers.

Too late, I realized that I was surrounded by hunters. One had his javelin pointed at my throat. The minute I felt the cool blade of his javelin on my throat, I went limp. While I was falling, I felt a hound nip at my back. I felt warm blood trickling down my back and from the surface wound on my neck. The streams of warm blood tickled me.

But I succeeded in playing dead. The tapestry doesn't depict this, but I remember being rolled onto a kind of gurney, made with a woven cloth in between two long wooden poles. I could hear the heavy grunting of the men under me as they lifted me up. I imagined them hoisting the wooden poles on their shoulders.

"Finally," said one of the hunters. His voice was deep and guttural. "The king will reward us handsomely now that the unicorn is dead."

That's how I knew my plan had worked. The hunters thought they had killed me. I remember thinking this as I kept my eyes closed and pretended that I was dead.

I imagined that it was a celebration of sorts as I rode above the hunters' shoulders to see the King. But I knew enough to continue to play dead. I could regulate my breathing. In fact, I had done this before when I was hiding — not only from the hunters but from the regular people who wished me no harm — I think. Or was it that they wished me no harm when they saw me because they were in such awe of me? In any event, it was obvious that the hunters thought there was a bounty on my hide, and they thought they had killed me.

Silly hunters!

It is I who outlived them all — even though they too are depicted in the tapestries, they are in the past and I am in the present. After all, here I am talking to you. And the hunters are just depictions of themselves. They are not real. They only look real. They look very cocky in their red velvet dresses and tights as they walk with their happy hounds to the castle. The nearby townspeople came out from their manors to view the spectacle passing by.

For some reason, it is the women that stand out to me now as I look at this tapestry. All are wearing headdresses. Many of the headdresses look like white caps on their heads with wide swathes of fabric hanging down to the shoulders of their fancy dresses. One with a red and white headscarf hanging down on top of her royal blue dress embroidered with shiny flowers is whispering to the woman next to her. This woman is wearing a white headdress that flows down on top of her red dress with an unusually low-cut bodice. I wonder what the first woman is whispering to her. Perhaps they are in love with each other, like the two women I spied in the abbey. But I doubt it. Towns consisted of manors. Even hovels were run by men who presumed themselves to be lord of the manor.

I had never seen these women before. I made a mental note to look for them in the future and to sniff the air around them and see if I wanted to lay my head in their laps. But now I know that it no longer matters. I have no sense of smell in the tapestry. Besides, I already had been captured — not only captured but killed. So, they thought!

I recognized some of the other women. I had lay my head in the laps of some of them, years ago when they were maidens.

There was one I remembered. Long before the time when I was playing dead and being carried to the castle, I had sniffed the air near a woman who looked just like her and kept on going. In the tapestry, she is standing with her husband — her "lord." It looks like she is telling him what they are going to do next. I can tell from their hands that she is in control. Her hands are pointed forward as if she is directing the way to where they are going.

His arm is looped through the arm of her golden-brown dress and resting at the waist of his pleated red dress. The more I stare at him, the more I think that he is not much of a "husband," with his fine features and long golden locks under his fur hat. Maybe they had an arrangement.

In any event, I do remember that she wasn't a virgin when I sniffed the air around her some time ago before she appeared in this tapestry. I have a very strong gut feeling that this was before she was with her fancy "husband" in his red pleated dress!

Who was she kidding? She hadn't been a virgin for a long time — probably long before she was married to her so-called husband.

Even now I can hear the ancient words echoing in my mind:

> *"Give heed then, you hearers*
> *and you also, the angels and those who have been sent,*
> *and you spirits who have arisen from the dead.*
> *For I am the one who alone exists,*
> *and I have no one who will judge me.*
> *For many are the pleasant forms which exist in numerous sins,*
> *and incontinencies,*
> *and disgraceful passions,*
> *and fleeting pleasures,*
> *which (men) embrace until they become sober*
> *and go up to their resting place.*
> *And they will find me there,*
> *and they will live,*
> *and they will not die again."*

Chapter Thirty-One

I digressed in thinking that the woman, who I saw in the tapestry, probably hadn't been a virgin for a long time and that it probably wasn't her husband who made her smell bad. Maybe it was a hired hand or a stable boy — someone she thought was "beneath" her. Maybe he was beneath her, physically, I mean. Maybe he had been on the bottom.

What does it matter anyhow? Rules are artificial and they are often designed to keep people unhappy. Perhaps the woman in the tapestry really desired the stable boy. And maybe they took pleasure in each other's company. Good for them! And maybe she really did lose her virginity to her husband. It seems unlikely that she would desire a match that was chosen for her. But there's a chance that it might have worked. If it did, good for her! I was just saying that looking at the tapestry now I distinctly get the impression that he looks like the kind of man who wouldn't marry a woman — unless he had to.

Rules are made by men to keep others in line. But if no one stepped outside the lines, life would be boring. For starters, what would the townspeople gossip about?

I realize now that my thoughts are a little bitchy. But I guess us unicorns are entitled to have our moments too. That is what makes us equal — that we can be just as important as others in our greatness as well as in our pettiness.

Now that I study the tapestry, I realize that there is so much I didn't see when I was laying on the litter with my eyes shut pretending to be dead as the hunters carried me to the castle to collect their bounty. The townspeople look as if they are gossiping to each other. It appears that there is a lot of furtive whispering going on. I wonder if they are talking about me. I think for a moment that they might be wondering if I am dead or not. But they don't seem too concerned. They're not even looking in my direction. They could at least be wondering who is going to collect the purse from the King, but that thought passes too. They are probably just talking about what affects them directly. Maybe they are discussing that their potatoes rotted this year and since it must have been the wrath of God, they are wondering who they can place the blame on.

There I am between the oak tree and the holly bush supposedly dead and being carried off so that the hunters can present me to the King. Everyone assumes I have died. On more than one occasion, I heard someone standing in front of a group in my room saying that the oak and the holly symbolize death — as if that settles it. The oak and the holly were everywhere in those days. Perhaps they do not symbolize anything. Perhaps they always just stood for themselves. But the guide always says these words as if they are final. Someone dreamed this up, so that's that.

I hear what they say as the groups, large and small, come through my room: "so sad;" "so depressing;" and so on. If I could talk out loud from my tapestry, I would tell them, "wake up! Don't you know, you can't believe everything that's told to you?"

I would say, "Don't you realize I am still here?

But I cannot get through to them — or, I should say, most of them. In order, for them to hear me, they have to first know they have been lied to and then believe that things can be different. If they believe, then they can hear me.

Belief makes room for me. Disbelief is a wall that shuts me out. This makes sense. Just think about it. If you don't think you will ever see me or hear me, you won't. If you don't believe in me, I don't exist — for you. But if you believe in your own goodness, then there is hope. For if you believe in your own goodness, then you can believe in me.

Recalling playing dead on that litter makes me think about mortality. As I stare at the tapestry, I realize that the tapestry maker never portrayed me as dead — or even playing dead. I am shown with the hunters' javelins going into my neck and another hunter stabbing me just above my haunches. So, the viewers assume that the hunters are killing me — and they are helped in their false thoughts with the wall sign that says, "The Unicorn is Killed and Brought to the Castle." But my head is held high. I look spirited and alive. Even my eyes are alert. I am never portrayed as dead. The viewers just assume the worst. But I am shown riding high on a litter. And the man in front of me, holding the nearest pole of my litter, is shown blowing his curved bone horn. He looks more like is heralding my arrival to the King or the townspeople – whoever will listen. For if he were heralding my death, wouldn't that be something to be ashamed of? Wouldn't all the hunters look ashamed? And the townspeople too?

But still this scene makes me think about mortality. People look at it and assume they know what will happen. Everyone dies, don't they? But do they? Sometimes people or beings die, but then they come back. Sometimes it seems like they are still here — or depending on how you feel about them — that they never went away. Sometimes species go extinct — like dinosaurs. We can't see the real ones because they are gone. But, in fact, they are all around us. Usually, they come back in human form.

Species don't come back human to human or animal to animal. The separation between human and animal is artificial. What matters is a being's connection to goodness. Sometimes animals come back as humans. Sometimes humans come back as animals. It's all the same thing. Goodness takes on light and then it inhabits form.

Consciousness is eternal.

Thinking back to my ride on the litter, I remember now that the birds were singing to me. They might have been finches, sparrows, crows, or all three. They might have spoken the same language or different languages, but they were united in singing for me mournfully in the ancient language that I still understand: *Monokeros, monokeros, monokeros.*

At first, I could pick out the different birds based on their sizes. The crow went first – cackling my name almost. She was announcing my capture to the other birds as only a crow could. I thought she would have begun with a gloating "I told you so," directed at me and referencing the day that she had said the hunters were looking for me. But I never heard this. It made me think about the fact that beings often miss the ones they used to ridicule when they were living. I'm sure it was sad for the crow to have one less creature to gloat to. But I came to the conclusion that it was more than that. The crow seemed sad to see me go — or rather to give the appearance of having gone. Since I was faking my death so well, some might have thought that it was my turn to gloat. I was surprised that I had tricked the crow and the other birds, but I was far from triumphant. For the birds had always been my friends too. It didn't matter that one had mocked me by calling me "that silly unicorn." I wasn't about to let that one incident turn me against them. They had always shown me the way. I had followed their calls and listened to their languages. It was the drunken birds that I saw zigzagging in the sky that had given me the idea about drinking from the fermented pomegranates on the ground. I would always be grateful for that. In my own way, I silently lamented the loss of my freedom in interacting with the birds. For I was no longer picking up my head and cocking my ears as I lay on the litter. I was pretending to be dead and who knew what that would lead to. The crow's call was high and shrill and then persistent in case the other birds weren't listening. She told them the hunters had killed me. Then she said such nice things about me that I was shocked. She called me elegant and noble. She said that I spread joy wherever I went. She said the other creatures left me alone because they knew that was what I wanted. Then she said that I held the world together.

The other birds heard her. I could hear the highs and lows and it sounded like the different size birds were harmonizing. They started out singing fast but quickly slowed down. When they slowed down, I could hear that they were singing my name: — *m o n – o – k e r o s, m o n – o – k e r o s.* They were saying my name mournfully — in long syllables and at a low register like a dirge. I was surprised that I fooled all the birds — and not just the boastful crow. But most birds take their cues from humans, so they saw the hunters and the litter and me laying on it with my eyes shut and assumed the worst. That's why they were singing mournfully. Some might think I would feel proud of myself for having tricked them. But I didn't. For even if they honored the falcon above all others of their kind because he was the companion of man, they were still my fellow creatures. My memory makes me feel melancholy. For the first time, perhaps, I feel a little lonely. It's a new feeling for me. Usually, I like being the only one.

But now I remember, the birds calling softly, mournfully (as if I were someone they had identified as a kindred spirit despite that they had called me "silly"):

M o n o – k e r o s, m o n o – k e r o s, m o n o – k e r o s.

The birds knew my name and that meant something. I knew that I was beautiful, fine and good. But if I hadn't been so alluring, perhaps I wouldn't have been on the litter playing dead so the hunters wouldn't really kill me. Now I can't help wondering. What would life have been like if there were more of my kind? Would I have had companions? Would things have turned out differently?

Chapter Thirty-Two

"Have you heard? The hunters finally killed the unicorn," announced Peter.

He handed me the bucket of pig slop so that I could carry it to the trough in the pen.

Shorter than me, Peter was also a monk. His auburn hair hung in his eyes over his pasty dinner plate of a face. He was just as homely as me – if not more so. But he had an air of entitlement about him. I don't know where he got it, but he seemed to think he deserved the world. He was a notorious gossip. And he usually wasn't right. I ignored most of what he said. But this time, he got my attention.

"What!? I've been looking for her. When did the hunters capture her?" I asked.

Peter eyed me strangely. "Just yesterday. I saw for myself. The hunters carried the dead unicorn on a litter through the abbey. I asked one where they were taking her. He told me they were going to the castle to collect the reward from the King."

"Are you sure you saw her?" I asked.

Peter looked puzzled. "It was a unicorn all right. I looked over and saw his long pointy horn. I saw a hunter eyeing the horn too. I bet he was thinking that it would fetch a pretty penny. Unicorn horns are all the rage."

I grew angry and impatient. My hands were trembling. I put the bucket of pig slop down on the ground to avoid spilling it.

"But are you sure it was her?"

I gaped at him. I couldn't believe what I was hearing. Surely this was one of Peter's fabrications.

"I saw a unicorn if that is what you are referring to as 'she,'" replied Peter crossly.

I nodded.

"Why are you referring to him as 'she' — and what did you mean before when you said, 'you were looking for her?'"

I thought quickly. If I didn't think of something fast, Peter would be spreading rumors around the abbey that I was obsessed with the unicorn who I thought was female.

"Did I say 'she'? I meant to say 'he' — everyone knows that animals are usually referred to as 'he,'" I said and then added, "I must be spending too much time in silent contemplation and I can't get my words out right."

Peter eyed me suspiciously. "All right, I can understand that. But what did you mean earlier when you said that you had been 'looking for her?'"

I couldn't tell him the whole story — he'd twist it around somehow. "I just meant that I had heard about the unicorn and I was looking for him. Don't all monks look for unicorns?"

Peter rolled his eyes. "No," he said.

Peter smiled smugly. Blotchy freckles on his nose flared in the morning sunlight.

"I've never looked for a unicorn," he stated. "In fact, I didn't believe they existed until I saw the dead unicorn this morning being carried on the litter."

"Dead!? Are you sure? I always heard that it was impossible for hunters to kill a unicorn," I replied.

"I saw him myself — dead. Dead as a doornail. Don't be upset. The unicorn is just a dumb animal. There's nothing to be concerned about."

Nothing to be concerned about?! My beloved unicorn had been killed and it was all my fault. I felt like I was going to be sick. I felt ill, but I also felt mean — like it would help to take out my angst on Peter. I knew it wouldn't help solve anything — but maybe it would make me feel better for a quick moment. He really did look like he didn't want me to be upset, but he was still smug. Ordinarily, I would've let this go, been silent and bowed to him inwardly and wished him well. But under the circumstances I couldn't let it go.

"The unicorn is not 'just a dumb animal' as you say. In fact, the unicorn symbolizes Jesus. The Priest told me so. That's why I always looked for the unicorn."

Peter's smug look turned to one of dismay. His round pale face looked like someone had pricked it with a pin and let all the air out. I was glad my plan had worked, but at the same time I saddened to see my fellow monk like this.

"I was just being a good monk," I said to him, humbly.

Peter nodded and said, "Of course, brother."

He looked at me levelly for a moment, but then his look turned to one of piety.

I should've walked away then, before he had a chance to continue.

"But I'm sure the Priest told you that 'symbolizing' Jesus and being Jesus are two different things. We actually can't see Jesus — no matter how hard we wish, even if that wishing causes us to fancy that we see rare creatures."

I could feel my face turning red. Anger was rising.

He didn't stop there.

"But if the Priest says that the unicorn symbolizes Jesus, that must be why the Bishop was so intent on the unicorn being caught."

I raised my eyebrows in anticipation of asking a question. "But if the unicorn is — or was — a symbol of Jesus Christ, then why would the Bishop want the hunters to kill him?"

"But – don't you see," replied Peter – he was so excited that he let the bucket he was supposed to be filling, clang emptily to the ground – "If the unicorn symbolized Jesus, then the Bishop would want him gone, because we can't have graven images being worshipped."

"Oh." I looked down at my dusty big toe poking out of my sandal under my brown robe.

That must have been what the Priest meant when he had talked about false idols and narrowed his eyes at me. In his eyes, I was committing heresy by loving the unicorn. I could hear the Bible verse, from Exodus, in my head: *"Thou shalt have no other gods before me. Thou shalt not make unto thee any graven image, or any likeness of anything that is in heaven above, or that is in the earth beneath, or that is in the water under the earth."*

So, my devotion to the unicorn — and no doubt the devotion of others — made the unicorn a graven image. She was nature itself; she was the essence of light; she was everything to me. The few times, I had seen her I was filled with grace and awe. She was more important to me than anything — including God and his son, Jesus. Because of the unicorn, I knew what devotion was. Now she was dead. It was my fault.

I glared at Peter. Apparently, word had gotten around that the Bishop wanted the hunters to catch the unicorn. I didn't care if the Bishop had mentioned me or not. In fact, I preferred that he didn't bring my name into it. Who was I anyway? Just a lowly monk. The Bishop could take all the glory.

Peter did not take my silence and my angry countenance as a reason to be silent. I could tell that he was full of himself again. He would never consider the fact that he would probably be better off if he remained silent.

"And if the Priest said this about the unicorn, no wonder the King is offering a reward. I bet it is a handsome one. Say that isn't why you were looking for the unicorn is it — for the reward?" Peter's eyes glittered. "If you did, you'd have to hand it over to the Bishop."

"No, that was not why I was looking for the unicorn," I replied flatly.

"Yes, we have taken a vow of poverty," said Peter, almost contritely.

For some reason — maybe it was the thought of what had fallen to my beloved unicorn — I felt great sadness when I looked at Peter.

"Yes, we have," I replied. "We have taken the vow of poverty because if we have nothing, then it is less likely we will be greedy."

With that, I turned my back on Peter, picked up my pail of pig slop and walked toward the wooden pen with the pink snouts sticking out of the slats.

I did my best not to talk to Peter — or any of the other monks that morning. After I finished my duties, I walked aimlessly through the abbey. I still felt enormously sad. I couldn't believe that she was dead. Everything around me felt glum, too. I could usually feel nature smiling around me on a beautiful day like this. Instead, it felt like the trees were bursting with moisture that they would release later in a rainstorm when no one was watching. I looked up. The white clouds were darkening in the centers as if they were gathering the droplets that would allow the sky to cry.

Then I realized that the birds were singing a mournful song. I cocked my head and listened. It sounded like they were singing a Greek word. I stood still and listened intently. The birds *were* singing a Greek word. It was hard to make out though because the syllables were long: *m o n o – k e r o s — m o n o – k e r o s — m o n o - k e r o s.* They were saying the unicorn's name in ancient Greek. I became excited when I realized that I understood what the birds were saying. I realized that I was excited for two reasons. I could understand the birds — and I could understand the Greek! But just as fast, I felt contrite. I was guilty of the sin of Pride again. Look what had happened last time. My beloved unicorn was dead, and it was my fault. The birds were telling me something. The unicorn had been beloved to them also. She had been special, and now she was gone. The birds were sad and so was I. I walked on.

I had been headed to the library to study Greek, but I was way past the library when I remembered this. I was walking toward the East end of the abbey where it was quiet enough for me to think. The nuns may have had to take a vow of silence, but the birds didn't. They were usually chatting away down here, but all I heard was silence. The birds must have flown away. Maybe they were following the hunters and the unicorn to the castle.

Suddenly I heard female voices just when I was almost to the medlar bush. I stopped and hid behind it. I realized that I must have been walking in this direction for a reason. The whispering nuns who loved each other were like the unicorn. They were that rare. I thought it also was likely that they had seen the unicorn. I sensed that nuns in general and these two, in particular, were silent, spiritual people, who sat in nature and observed. Maybe it was because I had a mother who was so close to the earth — she could name each flower and fern and had pressed them into a book when she was young — but women seemed closer to nature to me than men did. Maybe that was part of the reason that I had referred to my beloved unicorn as "she." But even though I felt a little lonely and wanted to talk to them, I knew I couldn't. I didn't want to scare them.

I could just see the lower part of their white habits from my hiding spot behind the medlar bush. I was afraid one of the women would look over and spot my brown robe at the base of the medlar bush, but the two women appeared to be facing each other.

"It just isn't fair," lamented the taller one with the higher voice.

"What isn't?" growled the shorter one.

I heard some rustling.

"Oh, stop," giggled the tall one. "But in truth, Isabella, I do like it when you get amorous. I was just saying that it isn't fair that we have to be so secretive — that we have such a big love for each other, but that we can't let anyone know."

"Oh that," replied Isabella in her gruff voice. "But Heloise, think about it. We know that our love is special. We could never take it for granted — and we never would. For one thing, we know that it is ours alone to hold."

"I am not so sure," retorted Heloise in her soprano voice. "I would like to shout my love for you from the rooftops. I would like others to know that they could have the same love. I would like to be accepted by polite society. I would like to live happily ever after with you."

"But this is our happy ever after, my love," replied Isabella. "The flowers and the creatures in the abbey celebrate us. The sky smiles down on us. The clouds know our names. We are a family. You and me and Kitty. Where is Kitty anyway? I haven't seen her in a while."

"You and that ca –" replied Heloise. She sounded exasperated, but then she changed her tone. Don't worry about Kitty.
I saw her earlier among the Mary flowers. She was wiggling her
haunches and was ready to pounce on something… maybe a
mouse. I called her, but she ignored me."

Isabella chuckled and then spoke. "See — she is intent
on doing her job. And our job is to love each other. We have
something special Heloise. And the fact that we have to be
secretive just makes our love stronger. Believe me, we don't
need the acceptance of polite society. We were both raised in
it, and we know that people usually aren't really happy. They
just pretend to be. If we could live among them, they would
be envious of us and instigate all types of problems."

"Mmm. I think that maybe you have something there,"
said Heloise. "Maybe the envy of people who aren't really happy
themselves but pretend that they are is the biggest problem. If
they were truly happy, then they would have no need to envy
us – and they could leave us alone."

Chapter Thirty-Three

That afternoon after I had spied on the nuns, I was sitting in the Priest's office feeling guilty. I must have looked as glum as I felt, because the Priest asked me what was wrong.

"I heard the hunters killed the unicorn and carried her on a litter to the castle to collect their reward from the King," I said.

The Priest merely raised his eyebrows. His lack of surprise made me suspect that he already knew.

"The Bishop will be happy." This was all that Priest said — as if that was all that mattered.

"I feel horribly guilty," I blurted out. I had meant to keep my feelings to myself, but I could not contain them. I felt my bottom lip tremble.

"But I thought this is what you wanted. You've been telling me that the unicorn was real. Now you have proof. Maybe the Bishop will reward you."

"But now I don't care about all of that. I feel horrible," I replied. I paused for a moment to gulp down air. "It is because of me that the hunters were able to track her down and kill her."

"Don't take everything so personally," cautioned the Priest. He looked sad and bored. I swear he rolled his eyes. "This isn't about you. The hunters just happened to be able to kill him. Think of it as God's will."

"You mean that God predestined that the hunters would kill the unicorn. But why would He do that? I don't understand." I was filled with confusion.

"The most important commandment in the Bible — the first — says, 'Thou shalt have no other gods before me,'" said the Priest. He looked like he could recite the commandments in his sleep. He appeared to be that bored and tired. He looked sad too — and I didn't think he was sad because the hunters had killed the unicorn. I wondered if he had a lover's quarrel with Thomas.

I nodded. I didn't know what to say. Quoting the Bible to me wasn't helping. I still felt horrible — maybe more so if that were possible.

"You should be happy the unicorn was finally killed. Not only did you prove your point to me and the Bishop. The unicorn really does exist — or rather he did." The priest smirked at this as if my misery was a private joke to him.

I just looked at him glumly. I had never felt so miserable.

"Look, you're causing your own suffering," the Priest continued. "You should celebrate the fact that now you can move on. You can put this creature behind you and start anew by worshipping the true God instead of committing heresy."

I stared at him. I had no response. When the unicorn was alive, it didn't feel like I was committing heresy by "worshipping" her. Whenever I saw her, I was filled with light, grace, and awe. The unicorn was the purest being I have ever seen. She did not deserve to be killed by the hunters.

I felt my bottom lip tremble again. I had to change the subject before I cried or had an angry outburst in front of the Priest. I scanned the book shelves. Surely, there was some kind of magic that could bring my beloved unicorn back to life. Alchemy! That was it.

"Do you have any books on alchemy?" I asked.

"Alchemy?! I thought I burned those books," exclaimed the Priest. "I would not have anything that could be construed as sorcery or witchcraft."

"But I read that Thomas Aquinas was given the philosopher's stone by his mentor."

I knew I was desperate. But if two plain metals can become gold and if there is a special stone that can make this happen then maybe I could still save the unicorn. Alchemy was said to be the elixir that leads to eternal life.

"It sounds like *someone* has been going to the library again. Learning is usually a good thing. But this is one of those time when too much knowledge is a bad thing. In fact, it is dangerous." The Priest paused and smirked. His eyes bugged out and his cheeks broadened as he pushed his lips together firmly before he spoke.

"Saint Aquinas, bless his soul, has been dead for more than two hundred years and in that time the Church has prohibited alchemy. As well they should. Not only is it an archaic and occult practice, it is dangerous."

"Dangerous?" My eyes felt heavy and dull like I was drowsy. But it felt like my sense of curiosity, was keeping me awake.

"Alchemy is said to have come from the Arabic part of the globe — the *Muslim* part of the world. And we know we can't trust the Saracens even when one of them agrees with us."

I raised my eyebrows.

"A so-called Muslim 'chemist' said that alchemy is not possible," the Priest elaborated. "He said that all that is possible is the illusion of change from one substance to another. But it always reverts back."

When the Priest said 'illusion,' I immediately began to think of the Bishop and his ruby ring. The philosopher's stone was said to be red. Maybe the ruby ring was really the philosopher's stone set in a gold band. Or maybe the ruby ring just created the illusion of the philosopher's stone.

But really what was the philosopher's stone?

Maybe somehow, the Bishop got the magic stone that was said to turn common metals into gold. It had to have been among Saint Aquinas most prize possessions. Maybe before he died, he gave it to a secret society. Maybe the Bishop stole it. Perhaps that was the secret to how he became the Bishop. Perhaps he was able to cast an illusion with his "ruby" ring. Maybe that was why I had betrayed my beloved unicorn. I was under the illusion that the Bishop could help me. I felt better thinking that it was the Bishop's fault and not mine.

The Bishop was just a mortal person, like me, like everyone. I looked at the Priest. He really did look sad. Maybe it wasn't fair that my sadness over the unicorn took precedence over whatever was going on with him.

I knew I had to choose my words carefully.

"You seem out of sorts. Did you have a disagreement with Thomas?"

The Priest gaped at me. He looked as though he couldn't believe that I knew what was going on with him. He paused as if he was going to reprimand me, but then he seemed to change his mind.

"Yes," he said miserably. "Things have not been good. I suspect that Thomas has taken up with Gregory again."

Then he composed himself. His look of misery turned to one of incredulity. His stern countenance — his eyes had become hawk-like, all seeing and piercing — let me know that HE was the teacher and that I was the student. I wouldn't think of prying further.

"Look," he stated. "I appreciate your concern, but I don't want to talk about this any further." The Priest paused and glared at me. "Before you interrupted me, I was going to say that people don't need alchemy — they have the Trinity."

"What do you mean?"

The Priest looked at me oddly.

"It's just assumed that you know about the Holy Trinity when you arrive at the abbey. There isn't a formal class taught about it," he said.

I bristled and felt something stirring in the pit of my stomach. Maybe it was fear. But then I realized that it was defensiveness. I didn't want my boyhood religious education to be found lacking.

"Of course, I know about the Holy Trinity. I just don't understand how it can be compared to alchemy," I responded.

"There are three elements that combine into one to create one holy element. Jesus is divine. His father, God, is divine. The Holy Ghost is what binds them together. But the Holy Ghost which is often symbolized by a dove, is a miracle by itself. We are reminded of that miracle on the Feast Day of Pentecost when a dove descends from the cathedral ceiling."

I didn't remind him that it was a *captured* dove that was shoved through the hole in the top of the cathedral and that dove did not come down of its own accord.

Instead I said "hmmm" and narrowed my eyes.

"Three's a magic number," I said. "People would be drawn to the number three."

The Priest raised his eyebrows and said, "I hadn't thought about that."

"Think about it," I answered. "Three is divisible only by itself and one. In many fairy tales, there were three questions. In Greek mythology, there were three fates. And in the Bible, there were three wise men."

"You're right," acknowledged the Priest. "Anything that attracts people to the Church is a good thing. It's no coincidence that we have three wise men. This is mirrored in the father, the son, and the holy ghost. Believers receive three divine gods in One."

"When I was young, I loved hearing about the Holy Ghost," I said. "My mother told me that the Holy Ghost was a spirit and that the spirit was female. I always thought that the Holy Ghost and the Holy Mother were one and the same."

Now it was the Priest's turn to narrow his eyes.

"The Trinity is made of three MALE divinities. The Holy Ghost is male – as is Jesus and God."

What the Priest said sounded lopsided. But I knew enough not to argue with him. He was, after all, the Priest. But I couldn't help blurting out:

"I guess my mother learned this from The Secret Gospels. And I may have gotten confused about the Holy Mother..." My voice trailed off.

"It's natural to want to defend your mother," replied the Priest sternly. "But remember that the *FORBIDDEN* Gospels are considered heresy. You don't want to fall into that trap again. Now that the unicorn has been killed by the hunters, you can renounce your ways."

"And you will give me back my epic?"

I don't know where the idea came from. But it was true that I didn't want my epic used as proof of my heresy. I glumly looked at the Priest and he nodded.

I sat in my chair and hung my head down.

Chapter Thirty-Four

Now that I am in my room gazing at the tapestry that portrays me being killed (supposedly) and carried by the hunters on a litter to the castle, I can ruminate on the scene. I have my memories, of course, but my eyes were closed. I remember that the trip seemed to take an eternity. I also remember that the terrain was very bumpy or maybe it was that the litter was heavy causing the hunters to keep adjusting the litter as they trudged under me. I heard the rough voice of one of the hunters swear as the litter lurched under me. But then it felt normal again — as if the hunter had lost his footing but regained it.

Given the legend that my kind could never be captured – that the wise old unicorn had told me about – you would have thought that the hunters would be happy. Even then I thought the hunters would have had a spring in their step, but no. They kept trudging along under me as they held the poles of the litter. I remember thinking that there must be a reason that they were hunting me. The king had most likely promised them a reward and they were taking me to the castle so they could collect it. But I remember that it didn't feel like anyone was happy, and now I can see that the hunters look grim.

Even their white horse, with a bit in his mouth, at the head of the procession has his head cast down. The hunter, now carrying his javelin over his shoulder, looks a little worried. Even the man stabbing me in my upturned neck with his javelin, does not have that look of glee — the bloodlust — that appears on the face of most hunters at the time of conquest.

The hounds — well they just look like hounds. These are relatively well-behaved hounds. But they are still surreptitiously sniffing each other's butts and their owners' hands — to make sure they haven't missed out on anything.

Perhaps the hunters are worried that they might not get their reward. Kings often promise riches that they never intend to give. Everyone knows that they are stingy and that is how they become kings. This would mean that the hounds wouldn't get their treats. Maybe the hounds picked up their owner's apprehensions. Hounds are so servile!

But perhaps I am being too quick to judge. For the hounds, like the horses, are creatures that are related to me. Sometimes I feel a kinship with some humans also — the kind ones. I suspect the unkind ones have been treated badly themselves. This is common behavior for non-human creatures, too. There's a good chance that we are all related.

But I digress. Perhaps the hunters are glum because they know that even if the King does give them a reward that it won't go far when divided among all of them. Maybe they are glum, because they know that if the King does give them a reward, it will barely mean anything to anyone. I mean that the reward will barely make a dent in the way the King lives and it will make even less of a difference in the daily lives of the hunters. They will come home with a leg of mutton or a pheasant that will last a day or two and that will be that. Maybe they are glum because they have realized that kings will always be kings and hunters will always be hunters. By this I mean that the King can afford to give out rewards (or promises) but the hunters will always have to work for their rewards. Not only that, but they will have to do the unsavory work of killing. Most likely, this is what their fathers did and what their brothers do. Since they were small children, they probably have been told that hunting runs in their blood. This might make them feel proud. They might want to be like their fathers (they certainly would want to please him) and they might want to fit in with their brothers. But I suspect a few would begin to understand that their father's life has foretold theirs, and it would be natural for them to feel trapped. They might pretend to like hunting. But who could like it really? To take the lives of innocent creatures is a despicable thing.

Maybe the hunters look grim because they are thinking about the fact that everybody dies — even them. And they are slowly realizing that if even I can be killed, they will probably die before their time.

It is even possible, that the hunters are glum because they like me. Maybe they realized at the last minute — when they thought it was too late — that I meant something to them. Even hunters recognize truth and beauty.

When I look at the tapestry, I see many beautiful colors. There are many shades of red in the pleated tunics, the form-fitting leggings, a low-cut bodice, the draping arms of a woman's dress. There are some interesting shades of blue too. One is so pale that it is almost silver, and it shimmers in the folds of the hunter's cape — the one in front with the horse, the hunter who looks worried. Another blue shoulder of a hunter's jacket glints at me. I see blue also in a woman's dress that breaks up the reds. The dress seems to have real flowers woven into it. At the bottom of the tapestry and the left side is a verdant shade of lush green overlaid with the lighter shades of herbs and small trees.

There are interesting shapes in the tapestry also. At the top right are the turrets of the town and the walls of the castle which is flying its flag. The flag is in the shape of a triangle. I am in the picture also, of course. There I am in the upper left-hand corner, providing a lively focal point. My head is raised, and I look like I am smiling as the hunters are supposedly killing me. It looks like I fooled them. Ha!

Even though I do make the tapestry more beautiful — some would say worthy of hanging on the wall — I can see now that the tapestry is not really about me. As I mentioned, the hunters look glum. If they lived now, people might even say they look depressed. (I hear people discussing their medications as they stand in clumps in my room.) And the townspeople are gossiping with each other. They are not even looking in my direction. They are just using me as an excuse to come out of their manors and try to outdo each other with their fancy dress.

There is one thing I notice now. Even though we are in sight of the castle, nearby really, the warrior princess is not in sight. I wonder if she will ever save me?

Chapter Thirty-Five

I've been looking at this tapestry for eons and really don't understand it. I would scratch my head if I could. I've even read the sign next to the tapestry — several times. It reads "The Unicorn in Captivity." The sign doesn't make any sense. I would never permit myself to live in captivity. Even if someone tried to force me, the circular fence around me is too low. I could simply walk over it. I wouldn't even have to jump. The chain that's attached to the wide collar around my neck is unbelievable. Why, I could break that chain with one jerk of my neck – as if I would ever allow anyone to put a collar around my neck!

It is the same scene that I saw the young wife weaving in her little house in the clearing. The only difference is now it is complete. Now I am sitting under a pomegranate tree. The tree has some thin initials around its thin trunk. I've heard it said that the initials (which are written in a thin script that makes it nearly impossible to make out) represent the letters of the names of the people who first owned the tapestries. But those people seem to have gone into obscurity. I heard one tour guide say that the tapestries were done by unknown artists for unknown royalty and several people in the group actually snickered. Then I thought about it. I decided that I would snicker with them if I could, because it is ridiculous to think that ownership of the tapestries — or of anything for that matter — actually meant anything. The tapestries are all about ME. To see my purity and to experience the awe and grace of their own purity and goodness is why people flock to my room and marvel at MY images.

Now that I look at the tapestry again, I see that the tree doesn't really look like a pomegranate tree. I have heard so many group leaders say that it is a pomegranate tree that my image is under, that I just took what they said as fact. But the trunk is tall, thin and bare — not gnarled and hidden in a bushy clump of leaves like most pomegranate trees.

There are no ripe red orbs — the kind that usually catch my eye. They are not hanging from the tree. But I see that there are pale yellow pink buds high up in the centers of the clusters of the leaves. Maybe these are meant to symbolize pomegranates that haven't yet grown or ripened. Logic would have it that the tree has not dropped any ripened and fermenting fruits on the ground. This is the only way that I could be domesticated — for a time. Because if I had drunk from too many fermented pomegranates, I most likely would be writhing around on my back and would not have noticed if someone built a little fence around me. But there is no red stain around my mouth to indicate that I have been drinking from fermented pomegranates. And I — or the image of me — is sitting upright, with my four legs on the ground. My head is erect and my horn leads up to the bottom of the so-called pomegranate tree. The little round wooden fence is not much wider than me and in the background is summer green grass with wildflowers everywhere.

I recognize the flowers — the sweet violet, the pastel pink primrose, the carnation with its white petals, the blue of the periwinkle, the purple iris, and the wild orchid's purple faded with time. Perhaps it is the orchid that I am supposed to identify with — for I was once wild and free and now appear faded and tamed with time.

But this is not true. I am still wild and free. Looking at this tapestry, I can only conclude that someone made up the scene. The image came from someone's imagination — so it is real to them and them only. They must have imagined that I could be captured, but that I would never die. On that last point they were right. They also must have imagined that I could be someone's pet. No doubt they thought that this tapestry would have to please whoever was paying for it.

I have no memory of what happened when they carried me to the castle. I do not know if the King did indeed reward the hunters. Maybe I blacked out. Perhaps whatever happened was so awful that I blocked out memory entirely. Maybe I escaped to some mountaintop where I am currently masquerading with two horns as a ram or some other creature.

I may be other places, but I am here too. I have been pondering this tapestry for a long time, but suddenly I realize something. I am sitting in a circle of the wooden fence. When people come into this room, they gaze at me sitting in the circle of that wooden fence.

Perhaps when they are gazing at the image of me, they have entered eternity with me in that instant.

What they probably don't realize is that they are standing in another circle of sorts — in this room. It is rectangular but, but it is still a circle in a way. They are standing in the circle of my seven tapestries. These tapestries prove that I exist. There was a time when almost everyone believed in me. Remember that, if you believe in me, and someone scoffs at you and says I don't exist. You don't have to tell them that you are right. In fact, insisting that you are right about anything, might make me go away.

As to who killed me, perhaps it is no one since I am still talking to you. But maybe someone *did* kill me. It could have been my young friend. But if he was not pure enough to see me — at one point — then you never would have seen me. Maybe I was killed — or was thought to have been killed — by the fear of difference. Or perhaps it was importance — or the need for the perception of it. I do not believe that importance is real for if we are all important — and we are — then no one is more important than anyone else. If one examines the need to be better than someone else, you will find that the only reason to desire importance, is that you feel unimportant.

I imagine that my young friend descended into guilt – which there is no return from – and that the Bishop faded into obscurity — despite his ruby ring and his sun-dial bracelet. As for the hunters, they are no more at fault than their obedient hounds.

The humans are gone, but I am still here. Don't get me wrong, I realize that I am not on the physical plane. And there are things that I miss about this beautiful earth that I love. Maybe what I loved most is the sudden and unexpected delight of fireflies on a warm summer night.

I hope to come back some day. Maybe the warrior princess will come rescue me. I have not given up hope. And neither should you. But do not be like me. Do not wait for the warrior princess to rescue you. Find your own warrior princess inside of you. Be her.

Heed the ancient words that still fill my mind:

"'I was sent forth from the power,
  and I have come to those who reflect upon me,
  and I have been found among those who seek after me.
Look upon me, you who reflect upon me,
  and you hearers, hear me.
You who are waiting for me, take me to yourselves....'"